"I have a proposition."

"Which is?"

Qadir smiled. "You may have noticed my father's efforts to interest me in a woman. He's determined to get all his sons married as quickly as possible."

"Typical father behavior," Maggie said.

"The only way to get him to back off is to give him the impression I'm involved with someone."

She nodded. "That would probably work."

"I'm glad you agree. So I propose an arrangement between us. We would date for a period of weeks. Perhaps three or four months, then say we're engaged."

She opened her mouth, then closed it. He couldn't be saying what she thought he was saying.

"I… You… It's…"

"A relationship of convenience. You will consent to be someone I become involved with for an agreed-upon period of time, say six months."

He wanted to fake *date?* Then get fake engaged to her?!

Dear Reader,

One of the best things about being a writer is creating characters who become so real I want them as friends. Maggie Collins is one of those special people. She's funny, she's flawed, she's very clear on her strong points and her limitations. She's the kind of friend who would loan you her favorite sweater for a hot date, then not be mad if you spilled salsa on it.

Her first experience with a handsome prince, who just happens to be a sheik, is a little disappointing. He's just a regular guy. Okay, a very rich, good-looking guy. And there's a teeny tiny chance he makes her heart beat faster when they're together. But she's just a regular girl from Colorado. Not exactly princess material.

So when Prince Qadir proposes a fake relationship to convince his father he's unavailable for an arranged marriage, Maggie goes along for the ride. After all, how often does a girl like her get to pretend she could actually belong to a prince? There's no way her heart is going to get involved. She's smarter than that...or so she hopes.

This is one of my favorite stories ever. I hope you enjoy reading it as much as I enjoyed writing it.

Susan Mallery

SUSAN MALLERY

THE SHEIK AND THE PREGNANT BRIDE

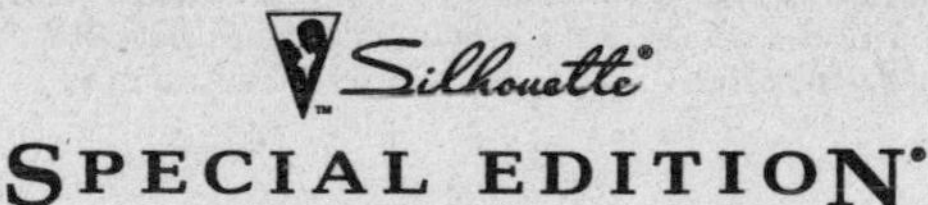

Published by Silhouette Books

America's Publisher of Contemporary Romance

If you purchased this book without a cover you should be aware that this book is stolen property. It was reported as "unsold and destroyed" to the publisher, and neither the author nor the publisher has received any payment for this "stripped book."

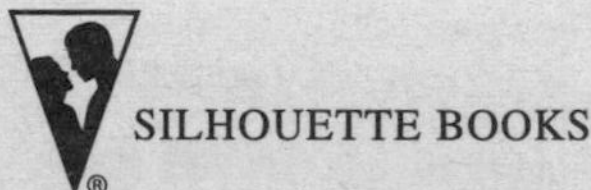

ISBN-13: 978-0-373-24885-8
ISBN-10: 0-373-24885-7

THE SHEIK AND THE PREGNANT BRIDE

Copyright © 2008 by Susan Macias Redmond

All rights reserved. Except for use in any review, the reproduction or utilization of this work in whole or in part in any form by any electronic, mechanical or other means, now known or hereafter invented, including xerography, photocopying and recording, or in any information storage or retrieval system, is forbidden without the written permission of the editorial office, Silhouette Books, 233 Broadway, New York, NY 10279 U.S.A.

This is a work of fiction. Names, characters, places and incidents are either the product of the author's imagination or are used fictitiously, and any resemblance to actual persons, living or dead, business establishments, events or locales is entirely coincidental.

This edition published by arrangement with Harlequin Books S.A.

® and TM are trademarks of Harlequin Books S.A., used under license. Trademarks indicated with ® are registered in the United States Patent and Trademark Office, the Canadian Trade Marks Office and in other countries.

Visit Silhouette Books at www.eHarlequin.com

Printed in U.S.A.

Books by Susan Mallery in miniseries

Silhouette Special Edition

Hometown Heartbreakers

The Best Bride #933
Marriage on Demand #939
Father in Training #969
Part-Time Wife #1027
Holly and Mistletoe #1071
Husband by the Hour #1099
Good Husband Material #1501
Completely Smitten #1520
One in a Million #1543
Quinn's Woman #1557

Lone Star Canyon

The Rancher Next Door #1358
Unexpectedly Expecting #1370
Wife in Disguise #1383

Positively Pregnant

Having Her Boss's Baby #1759
The Ladies' Man #1778
Her Last First Date #1831

Triple Trouble

The Girl of His Dreams #1118
The Secret Wife #1123
The Mysterious Stranger #1130

Brides of Bradley House

Dream Bride #1231
Dream Groom #1244

Desert Rogues

The Sheik's Kidnapped Bride #1316
The Sheik's Arranged Marriage #1324
The Sheik's Secret Bride #1331
The Sheik and the Runaway Princess #1430
The Sheik and the Virgin Princess #1453
The Prince and the Pregnant Princess #1473
The Sheik and the Princess in Waiting #1606
The Sheik and the Princess Bride #1647
The Sheik and the Bride Who Said No #1666
The Sheik and the Virgin Secretary #1723
The Sheik and the Christmas Bride #1862
The Sheik and the Pregnant Bride #1885

Silhouette Desire

The Million Dollar Catch

The Substitute Millionaire #1760
The Unexpected Millionaire #1767
The Ultimate Millionaire #1772
In Bed with the Devil #1815

SUSAN MALLERY

is a *USA TODAY* bestselling author of more than eighty romances. Her combination of humor, emotion and just-plain-sexy has made her a reader favorite. Susan makes her home in Washington state, where the whole rain thing is highly exaggerated and there's plenty of coffee to help her meet her deadlines. Visit her Web site at www.SusanMallery.com.

Chapter One

Maggie Collins hated to admit it but the reality was, she was a tiny bit disappointed by her first meeting with a real, live prince.

The trip to El Deharia had been great. She'd flown first-class, which was just as fabulous as it looked in the movies. When she'd landed, she'd been whisked by limo to a fancy hotel. Until then, her only other limo experience had been for her prom and then she and her date had been sharing it and the expense with six other couples.

Arriving at the exclusive Hotel El Deharia, she'd been shown to a suite with a view of the Arabian Sea. The living room alone had been about the same size as the two-bedroom house she'd grown up in back in Aspen.

She also couldn't complain about the palace. It was big and beautiful and historic-looking. But honestly, the offices where she was supposed to be meeting Prince Qadir weren't anything special. They were just offices. And everyone was dressed so professionally in conservative suits. She'd been hoping for harem pants and a tiara or two. Of course, as she'd mostly seen men, a tiara was probably out of place.

The thought of the older British gentleman who had shown her into the office wearing a tiara made her giggle. She was still laughing when the door opened and a tall man in yet another suit walked in.

"Good morning," he said as he approached. "I am Prince Qadir."

Maggie sighed in disappointment. Yes, the prince was very handsome, but there was nothing different about him. No medals, not even a crown or a scepter or some proof of rank.

"Well, darn," she murmured.

Prince Qadir raised his eyebrows. "Excuse me?"

Had she said that aloud? Oops. "I, ah..." She swallowed and then squared her shoulders. "Prince Qadir," she said as she walked toward him and held out her hand. "Very nice to meet you. I'm Maggie Collins. We've been corresponding via e-mail."

He took her hand in his and shook it. "I'm aware of that, Ms. Collins. I believe my last note to you said I preferred to work with your father."

"Yet the ticket was in my name," she said absently as she dropped her arm to her side, aware that even though she was five-ten, he was still much taller than her.

"I sent you each a ticket. Did he not use his?"

"No, he didn't." She glanced out the window at the formal garden below. "My father..." She cleared her throat and returned her attention to the prince. This was not the time to get sad again. She was here to do business. "My father died four months ago."

"My condolences."

"Thank you."

Qadir glanced at his watch. "A car will return you to your hotel."

"What?" Outrage chased away any threatening tears. "You're not even going to talk to me?"

"No."

Of all the annoying, arrogant, *male* ways to react. It was just so typical. "I'm more than capable of doing the job."

"I don't doubt that, Ms. Collins. However, my arrangement was with your father."

"We were in business together." The last year of her father's life, she'd run the car-restoration business he'd started years ago. And lost it, although that hadn't been because of anything she'd done wrong. The medical bills had been massive. In the end she'd had to sell everything to pay them, including the business.

"This project is very important to me. I want someone with experience."

She wanted to deck him. Given the fact that she was female and he was well-bred, she could probably get one shot in, what with the element of surprise on her side. But to what end? Hitting a member of the royal family was hardly the way to get the job.

"There were exactly seven hundred and seventeen Rolls-Royce Phantom IIIs built between 1936 and 1939, plus ten experimental cars," she said as she glared at him. "The earlier models had a maximum speed of ninety-two miles an hour. Problems started showing up early because the cars weren't designed to be run at maximum speed for any length of time. This became an issue as owners took their cars to Europe where they could drive on the newly built German autobahn. The company's initial fix was to tell the drivers to go slower. Later, they offered a modification that was little more than a higher-ratio fourth gear that also made the car go slower."

She paused. "There's more, but I'm sure you already know most of it."

"You've done your homework."

"I'm a professional." A professional who desperately needed the job. Prince Qadir had a 1936 Phantom III he wanted restored. Expense was no object. She needed the money he offered to pay off the last of her father's medical bills and keep her promise of starting up the family business again.

"You're a woman."

She glanced down at her chest, then back at him. "Really? I guess that explains the breasts. I'd wondered why they were there."

One corner of his mouth twitched slightly, as if he were amused.

She decided to push while he was in a good mood. "Look. My mother died right after I was born. I grew up in my dad's garage. I learned to change oil before I learned to read. Yes, I'm female, but so what? Cars have always been my life. I'm a great mechanic. If what they say is true, that classic cars are female, who better to understand them than me? I can do this. I work hard, I don't get drunk and knock up the local girls. Even more important, with my father gone, I have something to prove. You're a man of the world. You know what a difference the right motivation can be."

Qadir stared at the woman before him and wondered if he should let himself be convinced. If Maggie Collins restored cars with the same energy that she was using on him, he had nothing to worry about. But a female in the garage?

He reached for her hand and took it in his. Her fingers were long, her nails short. She was attractive, but not delicate. He turned her hand over and stared at her palm. There were several calluses and a couple of scars. These were the hands of someone who worked for a living.

"Squeeze my hand," he said, staring into her green eyes. "As hard as you can."

She wrinkled her nose, as if she couldn't believe what he was asking, then she did as he requested.

Her fingers crushed his in a powerful grip.

Impressive, he thought. Perhaps she was who and what she claimed.

"Should we arm wrestle next?" she asked. "Or have a spitting contest?"

He laughed. "That will not be required." He released her hand. "Would you like to see the car?"

Her breath caught. "I would love to."

They walked through the palace to the garage. Along the way, Qadir pointed out some of the public rooms along with a few of the more notable antiquities. Maggie paused to look at a large tapestry.

"That's a lot of sewing," she said.

"Yes, it is. It took fifteen women over ten years to complete it."

"I don't have the patience for that sort of thing. Seriously? I would have killed someone within the first six months. One night I would have snapped and run screaming through the palace with an ax."

The vivid image amused him. Maggie Collins was not a typical woman and he had met more than enough to know the difference. Although she was tall and slim, she moved with a purpose that was far from feminine. She had striking features, but wore no makeup to enhance them. Long dark hair hung down her back in a simple braid.

He was used to women using flattery and sexuality to get what they wanted, yet she did not. The change was…interesting.

"This is my first palace," she said as they continued walking down the long corridor.

"What do you think?"

"That it's beautiful, but a little big for my taste."

"No dreams of being a princess?"

She laughed. "I'm not exactly princess material. I grew up dreaming of racing cars, not horses. I'd rather work on a fussy transmission than go shopping."

"Why aren't you racing cars? Women do."

"I don't have the killer competitive instinct. I like to go fast. I mean, who doesn't? But I'm not into winning at any cost. It's a flaw." She pointed at an ancient Sumerian bowl and wrinkled her nose. "That's a whole new level of ugly."

"It's over four thousand years old."

"Really? That doesn't make it any more attractive. Seriously, would you want that in your living room?"

He'd never paid much attention to the ancient piece of pottery, but now he had to admit it wasn't to his taste.

"It's better here, where all can enjoy it."

"Very diplomatic. Is that your prince training?"

"You are comfortable speaking your mind."

Maggie sighed. "I know. It gets me into trouble. I'll try to be quiet now."

And she was, until they reached the garage. He opened the door and led her inside. Lights came on automatically.

There were only a dozen or so vehicles in this structure. Others were housed elsewhere. Maggie walked past the staff Volvo, his Lamborghini, two Porsches, the Land Rover and Hummer to the battered Rolls-Royce Phantom III at the far end.

"Oh, man, I never thought I'd see one of these up close," Maggie breathed.

She ran her hands along the side of the car. "Poor girl, you're not looking your best, are you? But I can fix that." She turned to Qadir. "The first one of these was seen in October 1935 at the London Olympia Motor Show. They brought nine Phantoms, but only one of them had an engine in it." She turned back to the car. "She's a V-12, zero to sixty in sixteen-point-eight seconds. That's pretty fast for this big a car. Especially considering how quiet the engine runs."

Maggie circled the vehicle, touching it, breathing in, as if trying to make it a part of her. Her eyes were wide, her expression one of wonder. He'd seen that look on a woman's face before, but usually only when giving expensive jewels or shopping trips to Paris and Milan.

"You have to let me do this," she told him. "No one will love her more than I do."

George Collins had been one of the best restorers and mechanics in the business. Had he passed on his greatness to his daughter or was she simply trading on his name?

Maggie opened the passenger door. "Rats," she muttered, then looked at him. "They've chewed the hell out of the leather. But I know a guy who can work miracles."

"How long would it take to restore her?" he asked.

She grinned. "How much money do you have?"

"An endless supply."

"Must be nice." She considered the question. "With express delivery and my contacts, six to eight weeks, assuming I can find what I need. I'll want to fly in someone to do the upholstery and the painting. I'll do everything else myself. I'm assuming I can get metal work done locally."

"You can."

She straightened and folded her arms over her chest. "Do we have a deal?"

Qadir had no problem working with women. He liked women. They were soft and appealing and they smelled good. But the Phantom was special.

"You can't refuse me because I'm female," Maggie told him.

"That's wrong. You know that's wrong. El Deharia is forward and progressive." She looked away, then turned back to face him. "My father is gone and I miss him every moment of every day. I need to do this for him. Because that's what he would have wanted. No one is going to care more about doing this right than me, Prince Qadir. I give you my word."

An impassioned plea. "But does your word have value?"

"I've killed a man for assuming less."

He laughed at the unexpected response. "Very well, Ms. Collins. You may restore my car. The deal will be the same as the one I negotiated with your father. You have six weeks to restore her to her former glory."

"Six weeks and an unlimited budget."

"Exactly. Someone on my staff will show you to your room. While you are employed here, you will be my guest in the palace."

"I need to collect my things from the hotel."

"They will be brought here to you."

"Of course they will," she murmured. "If the sun is a little too bright, can you move it?"

"With the right motivation." He eyed her. "I do not appear to intimidate you. Why is that?"

"You're just some guy with a car and a checkbook, Prince Qadir."

"In other words, a job."

"A really great job, but a job. When this is done, I'll go home to my real life and you'll have the sweetest ride in El Deharia. We'll both get what we want."

Qadir smiled. "I always do."

Maggie refused to think about how much per minute she was paying on her calling card as the phone rang.

"Hello?"

"Hey, Jon, it's me."

"Did you get it?"

Maggie threw herself back on the massive bed in her large suite. A suite that was even bigger than the one at the hotel. "Of course. Was there any doubt?"

"He was expecting your dad."

"I know, but I dazzled him with my charm."

Jon laughed. "Maggie, you don't have any charm. Did you bully him? I know you bullied him."

"He's a prince, which makes him immune to the whole bullying thing. Besides, I'm a nice person."

"Mostly, but you're also driven and determined. I know you."

"Better than anyone," she agreed, keeping her voice light despite the sudden tightness in her chest. Losing her dad had been the worst thing that had ever happened to her, but losing Jon had been nearly as bad. Jon had been her best friend, her first lover…pretty much everything.

"How's the car?" he asked.

Maggie launched into ten minutes of praise complete with technical details. She paused only when she recognized Jon's "uh-huhs" for what they were. Lack of interest.

"You're writing an e-mail, aren't you?" she demanded.

"No. Of course not. I'm mesmerized by, ah, the V-8 engine."

"It's a V-12 and I'll stop talking about it now. I should let you get back to work."

"I'm glad you got the job. Let me know how it goes. Or if you need anything."

"I will. Say hi to Elaine."

Jon didn't answer.

Maggie sighed. "I mean it. Say hi to her. I'm happy for you, Jonny."

"Maggie—"

"Don't. We're friends. That's what we're supposed to be. We both know that. I gotta run. I'll talk to you later. Bye."

She hung up before he could say anything else.

Despite the late hour, she was too restless to go to bed. Jet lag, she thought, knowing the twelve- or fifteen-hour time difference had messed up her body clock.

She'd traded in her pantsuit for jeans and a T-shirt. After slipping her feet into a pair of flip-flops, she opened the French doors and stepped out into the cool night air.

Her rooms faced the ocean, which was pretty exciting. Back home she had great views of the mountains, but vast expanses of water was its own special treat.

"Don't get used to living like this," she reminded herself. She'd rented out her house for the next couple of months. It was the end of ski season in Aspen and rentals still went for a premium. But once the job was done, she would be returning to the small house where she'd grown up, with its creaky stairs and single bathroom.

She breathed in the smell of salt air. There were lights in the garden below and the sound of voices in the distance. From what she could tell, the balcony circled the entire palace. Curious and eager to explore, Maggie closed her door behind her and started walking.

She passed empty rooms and a lot of closed and curtained windows. One set of doors stood open. She caught a glimpse of three girls cuddling on the sofa with a man who looked a little like Qadir.

A brother, she figured. From what she remembered reading, the king had several sons. No daughters. One wouldn't want a mere woman getting in the way, she thought with a grin. What would it be like to grow up here? Rich and pampered, being given ponies from the age of three. It must be—

"Qadir, I expect more," a gruff voice said in the darkness.

Maggie skidded to a halt so quickly, she nearly slid out of her sandals.

"In time," Qadir said, his voice calm.

"How much time? As'ad is engaged. He will be married in a few weeks. You need to settle down, as well. How is it possible I have so many sons and no grandchildren?"

Maggie knew the smartest thing would be to turn around and head back to her room. It's what she meant to do…except she couldn't help wanting to listen. She'd never heard a king speak to a prince before. She couldn't believe they were arguing, just like a regular family.

She slipped behind a large pole and did her best to stay completely silent as Qadir said, "As'ad brings you three daughters. That should be enough for a start."

"You are not taking this seriously. With all the women you have been with, you should have found at least one you're willing to marry."

"Sorry. No."

"It's that girl," the king murmured. "From before. She's the reason."

"She has nothing to do with this."

Woman? What woman? Maggie made a mental note to get on the computer and check out Qadir's past.

"If you cannot find a bride on your own, I will find one for you," the king said. "You *will* do your duty."

There was the sound of footsteps, then a door closed. Maggie stayed in place, not sure if both men had left.

She breathed as quietly as she could and was about to go back the way she'd come when she heard Qadir say, "You can come out now. He's gone."

Maggie winced as heat burned her cheeks. She stepped into

view. "I didn't mean to listen in. I was taking a walk and then you were talking. I was really quiet. How did you know I was here?"

Qadir nodded toward the plate-glass window that reflected the balcony. "I saw you approaching. It does not matter. My quarrel with the king is common knowledge. It is an argument my brothers and I share with him."

"Still, I wasn't eavesdropping on purpose."

"You seem intent on repeating that fact."

"I don't want you to think I'm rude."

"But I have already hired you. What does it matter what I think?"

"Because you're my boss. You could fire me tomorrow."

"True, but per our contract, you would still get paid."

She fought against the need to roll her eyes. "While the money is important, so is doing a good job. I don't want to leave until the car is finished. It's a matter of pride."

Maybe being über-rich and a sheik meant he wouldn't understand that. Maggie doubted Qadir had ever had to work for anything.

"Will your father really find you a wife?" she asked.

"He will try. Ultimately the choice is mine. I can refuse to marry her."

"Why would he think anyone would agree to an arranged marriage?"

Qadir leaned against the railing. "The woman in question will be marrying into a royal family. We trace our bloodline back more than a thousand years. For some, the dictates of history and rank matter far more than any matters of the heart."

A thousand years? Maggie couldn't imagine that. But then she'd grown up under relatively modest circumstances in a fairly typical medium-size town. Over the past few years movie stars showed up every winter to ski, but she didn't have any contact with them. Nor did she want any. She preferred regular people to the rich and famous. And to princes. Even one as handsome as the man in front of her.

"You must have all kinds of women throwing themselves at you," she said. "Aren't there any you want to marry?"

Qadir raised his eyebrows. "You take my father's side in this?"

"You're royal. Doesn't having heirs come with the really plush surroundings?"

"So you're practical."

"I understand family loyalty and duty."

"Would you have agreed to an arranged match if it had been expected?"

Maggie considered the question. "I don't know. Maybe. If I'd always known it was going to be that way. I'm not sure I would have liked it."

"Such an obedient daughter."

"Not on purpose. I loved my father very much." He'd been all the family she'd ever had. She still expected to see him in the house or hear his footsteps. One of the big advantages of her job in El Deharia—besides the money—was that she could escape the sad memories for a few weeks.

Qadir shook his head. "I am sorry. I had forgotten your recent loss. I did not mean to remind you of your pain."

"Don't worry about it. I'm kind of bringing it with me everywhere I go."

He nodded slowly as if he understood what it meant to lose something so precious. Did he? Maggie realized she knew nothing about Qadir beyond what she'd heard on television. She didn't read gossip magazines. Or fashion magazines for that matter. Her idea of a great evening was when *Car and Driver* arrived in the mail.

"You must have other family back in Aspen," he said. "How will they cope with you gone?"

"I, ah, I'm kind of alone. It was just my dad and me. I have a few friends, but they're busy with their lives."

"So you had no one to call and tell about your new job?"

"I called Jon. He worries about me."

Qadir's dark gaze settled on her face. "Your boyfriend?"

"Not anymore," she said lightly. "He's someone I've known forever. We grew up next door to each other. We played together when we were kids, then kind of fell in love in high school. Everyone assumed we'd get married, but it never seemed to happen."

She'd always wondered why they hadn't taken that last step. They'd dated for years, been each other's first time. He was the only man she'd ever been with and until Elaine, Jon had only been with her. She still loved him—a part of her would always love him.

"I think we fell out of 'in love,' if that makes sense. We still care for each other, but it's not the same. I think we would have broken up a long time ago, except my dad was sick and Jon didn't want to dump that on me, too."

But she'd sensed the changes in their relationship. "I ignored the obvious because of my dad dying. After he was gone, Jon and I talked and I realized it had been over for a long time." She forced a smile she didn't feel. "He's met someone else. Elaine. She's great and they're crazy about each other. So that's good."

She mostly meant that. Jon was her friend and she wanted him to be happy. But every now and then she wondered why she couldn't have met someone, too.

"You are very understanding," Qadir said. "Even if it is all a mask."

She stiffened. "I'm not pretending."

"You're saying there is no anger at Jon for replacing you so easily?"

"None at all," she snapped, then sighed. "Okay, there's a twinge, but it's not a big deal. I don't really want him for myself, exactly."

"But he should have had the common courtesy to wait a while before finding the love of his life."

"I can't agree with that. It makes me sound horrible."

"It makes you sound human."

"I'm emotionally tough." At least she was trying to be. There had been a single breakdown about five weeks ago. She'd called Jon, sobbing and trembling with pain. She'd hurt everywhere, not only from the loss of her father, but from the loss of her best friend.

Jon, being Jon, had come over to comfort her. He'd hugged her and held her and she'd wanted more. She'd kissed him and…

Maggie walked to the balcony and stared out into the night. Thinking about that night made her so ashamed. She'd seduced him because she'd wanted a chance to forget all that had happened in her life. And maybe to prove she still could.

At the time, he'd only known Elaine a couple of weeks, but Maggie had sensed they were getting serious. In a way it had been her last chance with Jon.

When it was over, neither of them had known what to say. She'd apologized, which he'd told her wasn't necessary. Things had been awkward between them. They still were.

"Life is complicated," she murmured.

"I agree."

She looked at him. "You're not going to get any sympathy from me, Prince Qadir."

"You're saying my life of wealth and privilege means I don't deserve to complain."

"Something like that."

"You have many rules."

"I like rules."

"I like to break them."

Hardly a surprise, she thought as she smiled. "Of course you do."

He laughed. "I still do not intimidate you. What was it you called me? A guy with a checkbook and a car?"

"Is reverence an important part of the job?"

"Not at all. You may even call me by my first name, without using my title."

"I'm honored."

"No, you're not, but you should be." He took a step toward her, then touched her cheek. "Do not mourn for the man unwise enough to let such a prize go. He was born a fool and he will die a fool. Good night."

Qadir disappeared with a speed that left Maggie gasping. She didn't know what to think about first. The soft brush of his fingers on her cheek or what he'd said.

She wanted to protest that Jon wasn't a fool. That he was actually a really bright guy, which was one of the things she'd always liked about him. Except she liked Qadir's attitude about the whole thing. She also enjoyed thinking about herself as a prize to be won…by a man who was not a fool.

Chapter Two

Maggie finished getting ready, then hovered by the door, not sure if she was just supposed to go down to the garage or wait to be called or what.

"Palaces should come with instruction books," she murmured to herself as she reached for the door handle. She might as well see if she could find her way to the garage and…

Someone knocked on her door. She pulled it open to find a pretty blonde about her age in the wide hallway.

"Hi," the woman said. "You're Maggie, right? I'm Victoria McCallan, secretary, fellow American and your guide to all things royal. Victoria, never Vicki, although honestly I can't say why. It started when I was little. I think I was in a mood and I haven't gotten over it."

Victoria smiled as she spoke. She was a few inches shorter than Maggie, even in her insanely high heels. She wore a tailored blouse tucked into a short, dark skirt. Her skin was perfect, her nails long and painted and her hair curled to her shoulders. She was the very essence of everything female. Maggie suddenly felt tall and awkward. Not to mention seriously underdressed in her jeans and T-shirt. She didn't want to imagine what Victoria would think about the coveralls she had in her duffel.

"You *are* Maggie, aren't you?"

"Most days."

Victoria laughed. "Welcome to the palace. It's great here."

"Is there a map?"

"If only. I can't tell you how many times I've been lost. We need internal GPS or something. They could implant us with a chip and track us." She wrinkled her nose. "On second thought, maybe not. Are you really here to fix a car?"

"Work on one. I'm restoring an old Rolls-Royce." She thought about going into more detail, but figured the other woman's eyes would glaze over.

"On purpose?"

"It's not going to happen otherwise."

"I never got the car thing."

Maggie looked at Victoria's perfect outfit. "I never got the clothes thing. I hate shopping."

"I shop enough for two so you're covered. Come on. I'll show you the way."

Victoria waited while Maggie grabbed her duffel.

"Do I want to know what's in there?" the other woman asked.

Maggie thought about her personal tools and coveralls. "No."

"Good to know. The El Deharian palace was originally built in the eighth century. There are still parts of the old exterior walls visible. I can show you later, if you'd like. The main structure is broken down into four quadrants, much like the interior of a cathedral, but without the religious implication. There is artwork from around the world on display. At any given time, the paintings alone are valued at nearly a billion dollars."

Victoria pointed to a painting on a wall. "An early Renoir. Just a little FYI, don't even think about taking it back to your room for a private viewing. It's protected by a state-of-the-art security system. However, if you insist on trying, rumor is they'll take you down to the dungeon and cut off your head."

"Good to know," Maggie murmured. "I don't know much about art. I'll keep it that way. How do you know so much about the palace?"

"I like to read. There's a lot of great history here. Plus I've been asked to fill in a few times when foreign dignitaries want a private tour after dinner when the regular tour staff has gone home."

"You live here—in the palace?"

"Just down the hall. I've been here nearly two years." She paused at a staircase. "Look at that hideous baby in the painting." She pointed to a large oil painting on the wall. "It's the easiest way to remember your wing and floor. Trust me, most of the other art is much more attractive."

"Good to know."

Victoria started down the stairs. "As live-in staff you're entitled to a whole bundle of goodies. Free laundry, access to the kitchen. I will warn you that you have to be careful with the food. You can really pack on the pounds in a heartbeat. I gained the freshman fifteen when I first moved here. Now I make sure I walk everywhere."

Maggie eyed her high heels. "In those?"

"Of course. They go with my outfit."

"Don't they hurt?"

"Not until about four in the afternoon."

Victoria led her downstairs, then along a long corridor that led to the rear garden. At least Maggie thought it was the rear garden. It looked a little like what she and Qadir had passed through the day before.

"Back to the kitchen," Victoria said. "You can call in your request at any time. They do post a menu online, so if you want to just order from that, they'll love you more. Everything is delicious. Unless you want to weigh four hundred pounds, avoid the desserts." She looked at Maggie. "Of course, you're probably one of those annoying women who doesn't have to watch what she eats."

"I'm pretty physically active during my day," Maggie admitted.

"Great. And here I thought we'd be friends." She pulled a key out of her skirt which, apparently, had a pocket, and passed it over. "You have private access. Very impressive."

She waited while Maggie unlocked the side door, then they stepped into the massive garage.

Victoria paused by the door as the automatic lights came on, but Maggie walked directly to the Rolls, stopping only when she could touch the smooth lines of the perfect beauty.

Victoria paused behind her. "It's, um, old."

"A classic."

"And dirty. And kind of in bad shape. You can fix that?"

Maggie nodded, already visualizing what the car could be. "I'm going to be searching for original parts, if I can find them. It will be a pain, but in the end, I want her exactly as she was."

"Okay, then. Sounds like fun." Victoria walked to a door. "This is your office."

Office? Maggie had expected a bay in the garage and a toolbox. She got an office, too?

The space was large, clean and fully equipped. In addition to the desk with a computer, there were bookshelves filled with catalogs and a wall-size tool organizer.

Victoria opened the desk drawer and pulled out a credit card.

"Yours. You are allowed to get whatever you need for the car. Qadir has placed no restrictions on your spending. I'm thinking you'll want to avoid a trip to the Bahamas, however. What with the whole beheading thing."

Maggie laughed. "Thanks for the tip. Is this really for me?"

"All of it. I was in here late yesterday and set up your computer. You're already connected to the Internet."

"Thanks." Maggie had been excited about the job before—working on the Rolls would be a once-in-a-lifetime experience for her. But to have all this, too, was unbelievable. "Guess I'm not still in Kansas."

"Is that where you're from?"

"Colorado. Aspen."

"It's supposed to be beautiful there."

"It is."

"How'd you end up in El Deharia?" Victoria asked. As she spoke, she rested one hip on the desk.

Maggie figured with those shoes, she would want to stay off her feet as much as possible.

"My dad had talked to Qadir about restoring the car. They were still working the deal when my dad got sick. Cancer. Things were put on hold, then he died and I decided I wanted the job."

It was the simple version of the story, Maggie thought, not wanting to tell someone she'd barely met that she had been forced to sell the business to pay for medical bills and that this job with Prince Qadir was her only chance of keeping her promise to her father about buying it back.

"I'm sorry about your loss," Victoria said. "That has to be hard. Is your mom still alive?"

"No. She died when I was a baby. It was just my dad and me, but it was great. I loved being with him in the shop and learning about cars."

"Well, I'm sure it's a handy skill." Victoria tilted her head so her curls fell. "So that's all this is about? A job?"

"What else would it be?"

"Marrying a prince. That's why I'm here."

Maggie blinked. "How's that working out for you?"

"Not very well," Victoria admitted with a sigh. "I work for Prince Nadim—he's one of Qadir's cousins. I keep waiting for him to notice me, but so far, it's not happening. Still, I have faith. One day he'll look up, see me and be swept away."

Maggie wasn't sure what to say. "You don't sound like you're madly in love with him."

"I'm not," Victoria said with a grin. "Love is dangerous and for fools. I'm keeping my heart safely out of the game. But what little girl doesn't want to grow up and be a princess?"

There had to be more to the story than that, Maggie thought. Victoria was too friendly and open to only care about money. Or maybe not. Maggie didn't have that many female friends. Most women were put off by the car thing.

Victoria glanced at her watch. "I have to get back." She bent over the desk and scribbled down a number. "That's my cell. Call me if you have any questions, or if you want to have dinner or something. The palace is beautiful, but it can be a little scary at first. Not to mention lonely. We can hang out."

"Eat dessert?"

Victoria sighed. "Yes, and then I'll have to take the stairs even more than I do. Good luck with the car."

As Maggie watched her go, she wondered if Victoria really meant what she said—about wanting to marry Prince Nadim. She supposed there were women who were more interested in what the man could provide than the character of the man himself. Not something that would interest her.

Unfortunately, thinking about men made her think about

Jon. She hated that she still missed him and that seeing everything around the palace made her want to call him. He would appreciate what she was going through. Knowing him, he would even understand her ambivalence about their situation now.

But calling wasn't an option. He was in love with Elaine. That fact shouldn't mean she and Jon couldn't be friends, but the truth was, things were different. They could never go back and she couldn't figure out a way to go forward.

"Don't think about it," she told herself, then looked at the credit card Victoria had left with her. She didn't enjoy shopping for girly stuff, but when cars or car parts were involved, she could really get into it. "So let's take you for a test drive," she told the card, "and see what you can do."

Maggie typed in the amount, held back a wince and pushed Enter on the computer. Less than a second later, her bid amount showed on the page. She clapped her hands, then groaned when someone outbid her by two dollars.

She wanted that part. She *needed* that part. Maybe she should just offer the full price and get the stupid thing now, without worrying about it.

Practicality battled with how she'd been raised and frugality nearly won. It was ridiculous to pay the full amount when she might be able to get the part for less. However, she did have to budget her time and as Prince Qadir was incredibly rich, she wasn't sure he would care that she'd saved him twenty bucks.

Still, it took a couple of deep breaths before she typed in the "pay this amount and buy it now" price. She writhed in her chair a couple of seconds before pushing Enter.

"Are you in pain?"

She turned toward the speaker and saw Prince Qadir stepping into her office.

"Is it serious?" he asked.

"I'm fine." She hesitated, not sure if she should rise or bow or what. "I'm ordering parts online."

"A simple enough action."

"It's an auction. I've been bidding all morning. Someone else keeps topping me by a couple of dollars."

"Then offer enough to push him out of the battle."

"That's what I did."

"Good."

"I probably could have gotten the part for less if I'd waited."

"Do you think that is important to me? The bargain?"

She looked at him, at his tailored suit and blinding white shirt. He looked like a successful executive...a very handsome executive.

"No one likes to be taken," she said.

"Agreed, but there is a time and a place to barter. I doubt there is a huge market for parts for my car, but what market there is will be competitive. I want you to win."

"I'll remember that."

"But you do not approve."

"Why do you say that?" she asked.

"Your expression. You would prefer to bargain and wait."

"I want you to get your car at a fair price."

He smiled. "An excellent idea. I appreciate the fairness of your concern. Perhaps a balance of both would be easiest."

He had a great smile, she thought absently. She hadn't spent a lot of time thinking about princes, but she supposed she would have assumed they were stern and serious. Or total playboys. She'd seen plenty of those during the season in Aspen. But Qadir didn't seem to be either.

"I'll do what I can," she said. "It's just I'm used to getting the best price."

"While I am used to getting the best."

With his family fortune, he always did, she thought humorously.

"Must be nice," she murmured.

"It is."

Maggie smiled. "At least you're clear about it." She rose and walked to the printer. "Here's a list of all the parts I've ordered so far. I'll start disassembling her tomorrow. I haven't seen much rust, which is great. Once I get her into pieces, I can figure out exactly what needs replacing. For now, I've just been ordering the obvious stuff."

She handed him the printout. Qadir studied it, even as he was aware of the woman next to him. She was an interesting combination of confidence and insecurity.

He knew from personal experience that many people were uncomfortable around him at first. They did not know what was expected. He'd asked one of the American secretaries to help Maggie get settled, but only time would make his new mechanic comfortable in his presence.

He reminded himself that being comfortable wasn't required for her to complete the job.

She was nothing like the women who drifted in and out of his life. No designer clothes, no artfully arranged hair, no expensive perfumes and jewels. In a way she reminded him of Whitney. There had been no pretense with her, either.

He pushed the memory away before it formed, knowing there was no point in the remembering.

"I'll want to pull out the engine in the next couple of weeks," Maggie was saying. "You told me you could help with that." She paused. "Not physically, of course. I mean hiring people. Not that you're not terribly strong and manly." She groaned. "I didn't just say that."

Qadir laughed. "You did and it is a compliment I will treasure.

Not enough people comment on my manly strength. They should do so more often."

Maggie flushed. "You're making fun of me."

"Because you earned it."

"Hey, back off. You're the prince. I get to be a little nervous around you. This is a strange situation."

He liked that she didn't back down. "Fair enough. Yes, I have a team you can use to pull out the engine. I have several local resources. I will e-mail them to you. Mention my name—it will improve the response."

"Do you have a little crown logo you put in your signature line?" she asked.

"Only on formal documents. You may have to go to England for some of your purchases. I have contacts there, as well."

"Any of them with the royal family?"

"I doubt Prince Charles will be of much help."

"Just a thought."

"He's too old for you, and married."

Maggie laughed. "Thanks, but he's also not my type."

"Not looking for a handsome prince? Some of the women here have exactly that in mind. Or perhaps a foreign diplomat."

Maggie glanced away. "Not my style. Besides, I work with cars. Not exactly future princess material." She held out her weathered hands. "I'm more of a doer than someone who is comfortable just sitting around looking pretty."

"That is the monarchy's loss."

She laughed again. "Very smooth. You're good."

"Thank you."

"The women must be lined up for miles."

He smiled. "There's a waiting area over by the garden."

"I hope it's covered. You don't want them getting sunburned."

As she spoke she leaned against the desk. She was tall. He

couldn't see much of her shape under the coveralls she wore, but he remembered how she had looked the previous day and was intrigued. Curves and a personality, not to mention humor. How often did he find *that* combination?

A flicker of heat burst to life inside him, making him wonder how she would taste if he kissed her. Not that he was going to. He was far more interested in her abilities as a mechanic than her charms as a woman. But a man could wonder…

He amused himself by imagining his father's reaction if he were to start dating Maggie. Would the monarch be horrified, or would he be pleased to see yet another of his sons settling down? Not that it mattered. Speculation was one thing, but acting was another—and he had no plans to act.

"I come bearing food," Victoria said as she stepped into the garage. "One of the cooks told me you never get away for lunch. He assumes you don't appreciate his culinary masterpieces. Trust me, those are people you *don't* want to annoy."

Maggie straightened and set down her wrench, then pulled off her gloves. "Thanks for the warning. I've been so busy pulling everything apart, I haven't stopped to eat."

Victoria set the basket on a cart. "Let me guess. You're one of those annoying people who forgets to eat."

"Somctimes."

"Then we'll never be really, really close."

Maggie laughed. "I think you're a strong enough person to overlook that flaw. Come on. Let's go eat in my office. It's cleaner there."

While Maggie washed her hands in the small bathroom, Victoria set out their lunch. She'd brought a salad with walnuts, arugula and Gorgonzola. Several mini sandwiches on fresh foccacia bread, fruit, drinks and chocolate-chip cookies that were still warm.

"I thought I was supposed to avoid dessert," Maggie said as she took her seat.

Victoria settled in the one opposite. "It's your fault. I had to placate the cooks." She slipped off her high heels and wiggled her toes. "Heaven."

"Why do you wear those if they hurt?"

"They don't all hurt. Besides, without them, I feel short and unimpressive. Plus men really like women in high heels."

Maggie laughed. "I've never thought about being impressive. And I've never tried to get a man that way. By being attractive."

"You could in a heartbeat," Victoria told her as she speared a piece of lettuce. "I would kill for your bone structure."

The compliment pleased Maggie. She'd always thought of herself as a tomboy. Girls like Victoria usually avoided her.

"How is it working with Qadir?" Victoria asked.

"Great. He really wants me to make the car perfect, which is what I want, too. I love not having a budget. It's very freeing. The progress is going to be slow at first, which he understands. I appreciate that. He's—"

She pressed her lips together as Victoria raised her eyebrows. "What?" Maggie asked.

"Nothing. I'm glad he's an excellent boss."

"That's what you asked me."

"I meant as a man."

"Oh." Maggie grabbed a sandwich. "He's fine."

Victoria laughed. "He's a sheik prince worth billions. He's one of the most sought-after bachelors in the world and all you can say is he's fine?"

Maggie grinned. "How about really fine?"

"Better, but still. You're really not interested in him."

"Not as anything but the man who pays me."

"Interesting. Then I guess you won't be angling for an invitation to the ball."

Maggie nearly choked. "There's going to be a ball?"

"Uh-huh. To celebrate Prince As'ad's engagement to Kayleen. They've been together for a while now, but no one was supposed to know. The official announcement was put off until Princess Lina, the king's sister, married King Hassan of Baharia a few weeks ago. Anyway, the ball is where the news is made public and everyone who works in the palace is invited. Apparently when the guest list is a thousand, what's a couple hundred more?"

"I've never been to a ball," Maggie admitted. Her only frame of reference was cartoons with princesses as stars and she hadn't really been into watching them.

"Me, either, but I'm very excited. It's sort of a once-in-a-lifetime chance to wear a formal gown and dance with a handsome prince. I'll be hoping Nadim finally sees me as a person and not his efficient secretary."

"But you don't love him," Maggie said.

"I know. I wasn't kidding before—love is for suckers. But if he offered me a sensible marriage of convenience, I sure wouldn't say no. I think I could be a good wife to him. Better than some of those plastic bimbos his father parades around the palace. Anyway, my point is, you should come to the ball. It will be great fun. You can tell your grandchildren about it."

Maggie wasn't exactly tempted, although the idea was a little intriguing. She'd come to El Deharia to get away, but also to experience something new in her life.

"I'm not much of a dancer."

"They lead, you follow. I have an appointment to try on dresses. Come with me. It'll get you in the mood."

"I don't think so. I haven't actually been invited."

"You will be. Ask Qadir."

"Ask me what?"

They both turned and found the prince in her office. Victoria started to stand, which told Maggie she should be doing the same. Qadir waved them both back into their seats.

"Ask me what?" he repeated.

"I was telling Maggie about the ball celebrating Prince As'ad's engagement. As all live-in employees are invited, Maggie said she would love to come."

Maggie scrambled to her feet. "I didn't. I'm not interested in the ball." She knew Victoria meant well but she, Maggie, didn't want Qadir thinking she was using him or their relationship. She motioned to the coveralls she wore. "I'm not exactly ball material."

Qadir nodded slowly. "Perhaps not today," he said slowly. "But I see possibilities."

"That's what I was saying," Victoria told him.

Possibilities? What did that mean?

Maggie told herself not to read too much into the word. Besides, what did she care about Qadir's opinion on anything but the car? He was just some guy. Royal, but still.

"I already have some dresses ordered," Victoria continued. "I could have them send a few more in Maggie's impossibly skinny size. With her hair up and in high heels, she could be a princess."

Maggie glared at her friend. What was Victoria up to?

"I agree." Qadir nodded. "Maggie, you will attend the ball."

With that, he turned and left.

Maggie waited until she was sure they were alone, then glared at Victoria. "What were you doing?"

"Throwing you in the path of a handsome prince. My quest for a royal connection has failed miserably, but that doesn't mean you can't be successful."

"But I'm not interested in him that way." She didn't think she would ever be interested in another man. Loving and losing Jon had been too painful.

"Can you honestly look at me and tell me you aren't the tiniest bit excited by the thought of dressing up in fancy clothes and dancing with Qadir?"

"We'll dance?"

"See! You're interested."

"No. It's just I've never done anything like that."

"All the more reason to do it," Victoria told her. "Come on—it will be fun. We'll both be fabulous and the princes won't be able to resist us."

Maggie had a feeling she would always be resistible, but allowed herself to momentarily wonder what it would be like to dance with a prince.

Chapter Three

"What is the longest river in America?" the guy on the radio asked.

"The Missouri," Maggie said as she undid the first screw in the window cranks from the door. "The Mississippi is the biggest, but the Missouri is the longest."

"Ah, the Mississippi," the contestant said.

"No, that's not it."

"Ha!" Maggie crowed as she set the screw into the small labeled plastic container next to her. "You have to pay attention in school."

"Or have a mind for trivia," Qadir said from his place at her desk.

She looked at the open office door and sighed. "You can hear me?"

"Obviously."

The American radio station in El Deharia ran a quiz every afternoon at two. She'd gotten in the habit of listening. Usually she was alone.

But today Qadir had stopped by to check out the parts list she'd put together. She'd sort of forgotten he was still in her office.

At least she'd gotten the answer right, she told herself. It beat getting it wrong.

Qadir stepped out into the garage. "You'll need access to a machine shop," he said.

"Along with a good machinist. I can explain what I want, but I can't make it myself."

She was rebuilding the engine rather than buying a new one. Unfortunately time had not been kind to many of the original parts and replacements were difficult, sometimes impossible, to find. She would buy what she could and have the others custom-made.

She smiled. "I'm sure you have contacts for me."

"I do."

"I figured. The thrill of being royal."

"There are many."

"I can't imagine."

"It is all I know. But there are disadvantages. My brothers and I were sent away to English boarding school when we were eight or nine. The headmaster was determined to treat us as if we were regular students. It was an adjustment, to say the least."

"Doesn't sound like fun," she admitted, grateful for her normal life. "Were the other boys friendly?"

"Some of them. Some were resentful, and eager to show us they were stronger."

"Bullies." She went to work on the second screw.

"Sometimes. My brothers and I learned how to fit in very quickly."

"At least you had a palace to come home to."

"And a pony."

She laughed. "Of course. Every royal child deserves a pony. I had to make do with a stuffed one. It was one of the few girly toys I liked. I was more into doing things with my dad than hanging out with the other little girls in the neighborhood. I hated playing dolls. I wasn't very popular."

"Until the boys got old enough to appreciate you."

He was being kind, or assuming something that wasn't true. Either way, she didn't know how to respond. That combined with a particularly stubborn screw caused her to slip and jam the screwdriver into the side of her hand.

"Ouch," she yelped and set down the screwdriver. Blood welled up.

Qadir was at her side in an instant, taking her hand in his. "What have you done?"

His touch was warm and sure. "Ah, nothing. I'm fine."

"You're bleeding."

Still holding her hand, he led her to the small bathroom and turned on the water. "Is it serious? Will you need stitches?"

Stitches? Just the thought of a needle piercing her flesh was enough to make her woozy. "Not if I haven't cut anything off."

She pulled free of his touch and shoved her hand under the water. The wound stung, but wasn't too bad. She managed to rub on some soap without screaming too loudly, then held still as he applied a bandage he'd found in the medicine cabinet. He was surprisingly competent at the task.

When he'd finished, he took her hand again and examined it. "I think you will survive."

"Good to know." Even not thinking about the needle, she felt a little lightheaded. How strange.

Maybe it was the bathroom itself. The space was pretty tight and Qadir took up a lot of room. But even all that didn't explain the sudden thumping of her heart or the way she couldn't seem to catch her breath.

She was aware of the flecks of gold in his dark eyes and couldn't stop staring at the shape of his mouth which was, by the way, a very nice mouth. They were close enough for her to inhale the crisp, clean, masculine scent of him.

He smiled at her. "You will be more careful next time?"

She nodded without speaking.

"Excellent. I must return to my office."

He released her hand and walked away. Maggie stayed where she was, her body oddly tense, her fingers tingling despite the pain from the cut.

What had just happened? She couldn't seem to focus and the few thoughts that did pop into her brain seemed unrelated to anything. The tiny puncture wound couldn't be responsible and there was no way she'd lost a significant amount of blood. It was the weirdest thing.

She looked toward the garage to where Qadir had stood only moments before. This couldn't be about him, could it? She wasn't attracted to her boss. It was a recipe for disaster. She knew better. And even if she didn't, she was still mourning the fact that she and Jon weren't together. She wasn't interested in anyone else. She couldn't be.

Maggie stared at the rack of elegant, sophisticated, *expensive* gowns and felt as if she'd stepped into a movie star's dressing room.

"I thought they'd be like prom dresses," she admitted. "These are real gowns."

"I know," Victoria said with a sigh. "They're beautiful."

"I can't afford them."

"Neither can I. Fortunately we get a discount."

Unless it was an ninety-five percent discount, there was no way Maggie could buy one of these dresses. She needed the money to buy back her father's business. She couldn't waste a few thousand dollars on a dress she would wear once.

"Still," she murmured, not sure how to explain to her friend that there was no way this was happening.

Victoria patted her arm. "You have to trust me. I don't want to endanger my IRA any more than you do. These are to give us ideas only. Then we're heading into the back."

"What's in the back?"

Victoria laughed. "I can see you're not going to trust me. Come on. I'll show you."

They walked through the elegant boutique with the plush carpeting and soothing music. At the rear of the store, they stepped past heavy curtains and found themselves in a plain corridor. Victoria walked purposefully toward a simple door. She pushed it open and then moved to the side.

"Prepare to be amazed," she said.

Maggie stepped inside. There were dozens of racks, all crammed with beautiful clothes. Pantsuits and dresses, blouses, skirts.

"I don't get it. Why are these here?" she asked.

"Consignment," Victoria told her in a low, amused voice. "The very rich and elegant bring their barely worn clothes here where hardworking young women can buy them for pennies on the dollar. How do you think I can afford to dress like I do? I get a four-hundred-dollar blouse for all of fifty dollars. You can find anything here and the quality is amazing. I love this place. Seriously, the evening wear is discounted the most because so few people have any interest in it. The stuff is practically free."

That was a discount Maggie could get behind. "They really have ball gowns here?"

"They have everything. Because I'm short and chubby, I'll

be buying used. You, on the other hand, are tall and willowy so you can probably squeeze your tiny butt into a sample. Not that I'm bitter."

Maggie grinned. "Willowy is a nice way to say flat chested."

Victoria wove through the dozens of racks until she found one with her name on it. She quickly sorted through the dresses and handed Maggie six.

"Now we try them on," Victoria said.

Maggie took them into the large dressing room on the left while her friend took the one on the right. As she pulled off her jeans and her T-shirt, she had trouble believing she was really trying on dresses for an actual ball. Three weeks ago, she'd been attempting to sort out her life in Aspen. How could so much have changed so quickly?

Unable to find the answer, she pulled on the first dress. It was peach, with a fitted bodice and a tiered skirt that fell in waves of shimmering fabric. Victoria ripped back the curtain and sucked in her breath.

"I knew you'd look fabulous. That dress is amazing."

"It's unusual," Maggie said, facing her reflection. She had to admit that the color was good for her, but she wasn't sure about the fluffy skirt.

"It's couture, honey, and when it looks that good, you say a little prayer. I, of course, am hanging out everywhere and will have to pay to get this sucker hemmed."

Victoria's dress was black, strapless and fit her like it had been painted on. Maggie did her best not to be bitter about the curves spilling over the top. But hemming would be required. At least six inches of fabric bunched on the floor.

"Nadim won't be able to resist you," she said honestly.

"Aren't you sweet? He's managed to resist me very well so far, but I'm not going to think about that. Instead I'm going to talk you into that dress. You'll be dazzling. I know you're not interested in Qadir, but there will be plenty of handsome, successful men at the ball. You can dazzle them instead."

For a second Maggie wondered if Jon would be dazzled. Then she reminded herself she wasn't going to think about him anymore. Not that way.

In truth, she didn't want to be involved with him. She just missed him.

"Uh-oh," Victoria said as she put her hands on her hips. "What aren't you telling me? There's a guy, isn't there? I can tell just by looking at you."

"There's no guy," Maggie told her.

Victoria kept staring.

"Okay, maybe there's half a guy."

"Interesting. Which half?"

That made Maggie laugh. "I mean I'm only half involved. Or less, even. I keep telling myself Jon is just a habit."

"A bad one, I'm guessing."

"We grew up next door to each other, so I've known him all my life. In high school, we started dating. Everyone assumed we would always be together."

"Including you," Victoria said.

Maggie nodded. "Then we started drifting apart. I think we both sensed the change, but neither of us wanted to be the first one to say anything. Then my dad got sick. By then we knew it was over, but Jon didn't want to break up while I was dealing with my dad's death, so the relationship went on longer than it should have."

She drew in a breath. "The thing is, we've been best friends forever. That's the part that's hard to give up. I miss talking to him. But he's with someone else and the truth is, we're not best friends anymore."

Victoria gave her a hug. "I'm sorry. That has to be hard. You lost your guy and your dad so close together. It's okay to take the time to deal with that."

"I know. I'm just ready to be over him."

"Love sucks the big one," Victoria said firmly. "It's why I'm never giving away my heart. I want a sensible arrangement with a man who is all about security and convention."

Maggie was surprised. Victoria seemed spontaneous and fun loving. "Won't that be boring for you?"

"Nope. I want safe and practical. Did you know it's a really big deal for a prince to divorce? So they never do. I like that in a man."

"Part of Nadim's charm?" Maggie asked.

Her friend nodded. "A lot of it. Plus, my dad can be…difficult." Victoria shrugged. "Having a prince on my side would really help."

Maggie sensed there were a lot of secrets in Victoria's past, but she didn't want to pry. The other woman would tell her when she was ready.

"I'm going to think about not making a fool of myself," Maggie muttered. "Is there a book or brochure telling us how we're supposed to act and stuff, because I could use some pointers."

Victoria grinned. "I'll see what I can find. It will be practice for when we attend the wedding."

A royal wedding? "I don't think I'll still be here," Maggie told her. "I should have the car done in less than two months."

"The wedding is in six weeks. Apparently As'ad is very anxious to claim his bride. So you'll get to be there. If nothing else, you can fly back to dance at mine."

Standing in the dressing area of her suite, Maggie stared at the peach dress practically floating on the hanger. Victoria *had* been right. It was the perfect choice.

On the floor by the fluffy hem was a shopping bag containing a pair of high-heeled sandals and an evening bag, also purchased from the consignment room at the boutique.

"I'm really going to a royal ball," Maggie murmured to herself, unable to believe it was happening. She was just some mechanic from Colorado. Stuff like that didn't happen to her.

She tucked her hands into her pockets to keep herself from reaching for the phone. The need to call Jon was powerful and she wanted to resist. While they had both claimed they would always be friends, the truth was, they weren't. Not the way they had been.

Everything was different and there was no going back. Everything was—

The phone rang. Maggie jumped, then walked into the living room and picked up the receiver.

"Hello?"

"You're hard to track down."

The familiar voice stole the strength from her legs. She sank onto the sofa and tried to remember to breathe.

"Jon. Is everything okay?"

"Sure. I'm calling to check on you. I haven't heard from you and wanted to make sure everything was all right."

"I'm fine," she told him. "Everything is fine."

Which it was—so why was she suddenly fighting tears?

Probably the loneliness, she told herself. She missed her dad and she missed Jon.

"You sure?" he asked.

"Of course. Work on the car is going really well and you'll never guess. There's going to be a royal ball here, and I've been invited."

"Good for you."

"It's kind of a strange thing, but I think it will be fun. And I've made a few friends. There's a great secretary here who is also

American. We've been hanging out together." Maggie talked a little more about her life then said, "How are things there?"

"Busy. It's quarterly season and you know what that means."

She did. Jon was a corporate accountant. While she couldn't relate to his world of numbers and reports, she knew he liked it.

"How's Elaine?" she asked, because the alternative was to say that she missed him and she refused to go there.

He hesitated. "Maggie, I…"

"I'm allowed to ask and you're supposed to answer," she told him. "Don't we at least have that much left?"

"It's not that. I hate how things ended between us. I want it to be better and I'm not sure talking about Elaine is the best way for that to happen."

Heat burned on her cheeks. She knew he was thinking about the last night they'd been together. When she'd called him sobbing about her father and he'd come over, because that's the kind of man he was. Then she'd kissed him and…

She pushed the memory away. In theory, they were equally at fault. It wasn't as if Jon had said no. But somehow she always felt that she was the one to blame.

"I've let it go," she told him and realized she meant it. She still felt stupid, but she wasn't longing for a repeat performance. "You've let it go. We're moving on. So answer the question. How's Elaine?"

"Good. Great. We're spending a lot of time together."

She could hear his affection in his voice. Maybe it was more than affection; maybe it was love.

"I'm glad," she said firmly. "You deserve someone great in your life."

"You, too. But watch out for those princes at the ball. They play by different rules."

That made her smile. "I'm hardly in danger, Jon."

"You're exactly what they're looking for."

She glanced at her scarred hands and thought about the long days she spent in a garage working on cars. She doubted a lot of princes dreamed about a woman like her. "If you say so."

They talked for a few more minutes, then said goodbye and hung up. As Maggie replaced the phone, she realized she didn't hurt as much as she thought she would. That talking to him had actually been…nice.

She probed her heart, trying to figure out if she had regrets that things were over between them. There was tenderness there, but it was a whole lot more about missing her friend than missing her lover. Maybe she hadn't been lying when she'd said they'd both moved on. And wouldn't that be a good thing?

"They're not comfortable," Maggie grumbled as Victoria rolled her hair with heated curlers.

"Beauty is pain. Suck it up, honey."

Maggie eyed her friend. Victoria was a blond stunner, with her hair piled on top of her head and makeup emphasizing her beautiful features.

"So you practically had to cut off a leg to look like that?" Maggie teased.

Victoria laughed. "What a sweet thing to say. Hold on to that thought because when I'm done with your hair, I'm going to pluck your eyebrows."

"I don't think so."

"You're going to have to trust me."

An hour later Maggie stared at herself in the mirror. "Wow."

"I know. You had all that potential just lurking. Maybe now you'll take a second or two and put on mascara in the morning."

Maggie knew that was never going to happen, but she had to say she'd cleaned up a lot better than she'd ever imagined she could.

Her hair had been pinned up in a loose style that allowed a few curls to tumble down to her shoulders. Makeup made her eyes look big and her mouth all pouty. Victoria had lent her a pair of dangling earrings that sparkled, and the dress fit her perfectly, emphasizing the few curves she had.

"I like it," she said slowly, then shifted her weight and winced. "But the shoes are killing me and don't say beauty is pain again."

"You'll get used to them." Victoria linked arms with her and stared at their reflection. "Damn. I'm still short."

"You're gorgeous."

"We both are."

Her friend was being generous, Maggie thought, but she was in the mood to accept the compliment.

There was a knock at the door. The two women looked at each other.

"It's your room," Victoria pointed out. "So I'm not expecting anyone."

Maggie walked to the door, nearly falling off her high heels as she moved. She opened the door and found Qadir standing there.

"Good evening," he said. "I am here to escort you two ladies to the ball."

Maggie stared at the handsome prince in his tuxedo. He looked perfect, but then he always did. "Really? That's so nice. Thank you. We're about ready."

She stopped talking and held in a groan. *That's so nice?* Could she have said something more stupid?

He stepped into the suite. "Hello, Victoria."

"Prince Qadir. You're looking especially royal this evening."

He smiled. "Thank you. You're both very beautiful."

Victoria grabbed Maggie's arm and pulled her into the bedroom. "You know he's here for you, don't you? I'm just a pity date."

"What? No. He's not. He's my boss."

"So he's carrying on a time-honored tradition. Be careful, Maggie. You lead with your heart."

Maggie rolled her eyes. "Please. Qadir isn't here for me. He's just being polite."

"Uh-huh. Do you see Nadim being polite and taking me to the party? Qadir is intrigued and when the man in question is a prince, you need to be careful."

Maggie appreciated her friend's warning, but there was no need. Qadir would never see her as anything other than his employee. Not that she wanted him to.

The two women collected their evening bags and returned to the living room. Qadir escorted them both downstairs and led them to the elevator.

When the doors opened on the main floor, she could hear music. There were dozens of people in the wide hallway, all moving toward the massive open doors at the far end.

There were lights everywhere. Bright chandeliers and sconces illuminated the well-dressed crowd. More people pushed toward them and Maggie found herself separated from Qadir and Victoria.

She didn't mind. Victoria's well-meaning advice had made her a little uncomfortable. Qadir didn't see her as a woman and she wasn't about to get any ideas about him. Sure, he'd been great about the car and he was easy to work for, but there was nothing between them.

She pushed Victoria's words to the back of her mind and concentrated on the beauty of the ballroom.

There was a dais at one end, with an orchestra playing. There were dozens and dozens of food tables scattered around the outside of the room with an equal number of bars between them. Guests pressed together, talking and laughing.

The women were so beautiful, Maggie thought, not sure where to look first. Regardless of their ages, they were stunning in amazing gowns and glittering jewels.

She reached up and touched the earrings Victoria had loaned her. The stones were glass, the gold merely a colored finish. But that didn't matter. No one had to know they weren't real or that she'd bought her gown on consignment. For tonight, she was attending a royal ball and she planned to enjoy herself.

She waited in line to get a glass of champagne, then sipped the bubbly liquid. People stood in groups around her, talking loudly. Some of the conversations were in English, but many were not. She recognized a few of the languages.

She moved closer to a large plant and wished she hadn't agreed to the high-heeled sandals Victoria had insisted on. She'd only been at the ball a few minutes and her feet already hurt.

Maggie glanced around to make sure no one was paying any attention to her, then she eased back behind the plant, slipped out of her shoes and bent down to grab them. She'd just started tucking them out of sight in the planter when someone came up behind her and said, "I'm not sure the king would approve."

She spun and saw Qadir standing behind her. His expression was stern, but humor gleamed in his eyes.

"They hurt my feet," she told him

"Then make sure you hide them so no one can find them."

She laughed and slipped the shoes under a couple of large leaves.

"Better?" he asked.

"Much."

"Have you danced yet?"

"No."

Before she could explain she didn't know how, he'd taken her glass from her and set it on a nearby tray, then led her toward the dance floor.

"I'm not very good at this sort of thing," she admitted.

He pulled her into his arms. "I am good enough for both of us."

He was warm and strong and held her securely. She rested one hand on his shoulder, her tiny evening bag held in her fingers. Her other hand nestled in his. He moved purposefully, guiding her with a confidence that allowed her to believe that maybe she *could* dance after all.

"See?" he said.

"Don't test me with anything fancy. Not unless you want people pointing and laughing."

He chuckled. "Are you always so honest?"

"Most of the time. I try to be."

"You are charming."

"Really?" The word came out before she could stop it. "Sorry. I meant to say thank you."

"So polite."

"It's how I was raised," she told him. "You're very nice, too."

"Less arrogant than you'd imagined?"

"Something like that. Although you have your imperious moments. Am I allowed to say that?"

"Tonight you can say anything."

Was he flirting with her? Was that flirting?

She wanted to believe it was. After spending her entire life as a tomboy, it was nice to be girly for once. Not that she would want to make a habit of all the torture Victoria had put her through.

"I like your country," she said. "The parts I've seen are very beautiful."

"The city is more modern than many parts of El Deharia. Out in the desert the people still live as they once did."

"I think I like my modern conveniences too much for that," she admitted.

"I agree. One of my brothers has chosen to live there permanently, but not me. I, too, want my conveniences."

They moved together in time with the music, swaying and sliding and turning together. She stumbled once, but he caught her against him. Then they were touching from shoulder to knee, pressed intimately as they moved.

She raised her gaze to his, not sure if this was allowed or appropriate. He was a prince, after all. But he didn't seem to mind and she found herself enjoying the contact, maybe more than she should.

It was the dance, she told herself. The night, not the man. But the faint tingles in the pit of her stomach warned her that maybe it was the man. Just a little.

"Are you homesick?" he asked.

"Not tonight."

"But other days?"

"A little. I think being here has been good for me."

"New adventures?"

She nodded. Tonight was certainly that.

The song ended. Maggie felt a jolt of disappointment as Qadir released her, followed by a distinct coolness. As if all the warmth had faded away.

She found herself wanting him to pull her close again. She'd liked being in his arms.

Victoria's words of warning flashed into her brain. While Maggie didn't agree that she led with her heart, she was smart enough to realize that regardless of how good Qadir looked in a tux and how much she'd liked dancing with him, he was light-years out of her league. All tingles aside, nothing was going to happen.

She started to excuse herself when they were interrupted by a tall, older man who looked oddly familiar.

"There you are," the man said. "I've been looking for you."

"Father, may I introduce Maggie Collins. Maggie, my father, King Mukhtar of El Deharia."

Chapter Four

K king? As in *king?*

Maggie stood frozen, not sure if she should curtsy—not that she knew how—or bolt. Worse, she was barefoot. She couldn't meet the king when she wasn't wearing shoes.

"Lovely to meet you," the king said, not even looking at her. "Qadir, I want you to meet Sabrina and her sister Natalie. Their uncle is a duke. British, of course. Well-educated." The king moved closer to Qadir and lowered his voice. "Pretty enough, they seem to have decent heads on their shoulders. Their older sister already has two children, so we know they're breeders."

Maggie still couldn't move but the shock had been replaced by humor. She was terrified that if she did anything at all, she would break out into hysterical laughter.

It wasn't just the king's matter-of-fact description of the two potential brides that made her want to giggle—it was the look of long-suffering on Qadir's face.

Apparently being a prince had more than its share of stresses.

When she was sure she could control herself, she eased back, pausing only to look at the two young women hovering just out of earshot. They were pretty, she thought humorously, and hey, known breeders. When one had to worry about the continuation of the royal line, that was probably important.

She was about to turn away when Qadir glanced at her. "You're not leaving." It sounded a whole lot more like a command than a question.

"Um, surely you want to dance with one of the duke's nieces," she murmured. "Sabrina is especially lovely."

"Exactly," the king said, smiling at her. "That's what I thought."

Qadir stepped closer to her and spoke quietly. "You have no idea which one is Sabrina."

"They're both very pretty. And reasonably intelligent. What more could you ask for?"

He started to say something else, but his father pulled him away.

Maggie took another step back as she watched the introductions. She was willing to admit to a slight twinge of envy, but this was for the best. Better to remember who Qadir was and where he was going than to allow a single dance to mess with her head.

Still, it had been a very nice dance, she thought wistfully. It had reminded her she was still alive and capable of tingles. Which probably meant she was nearly over Jon. A good thing, if a little sad.

She watched as Qadir spoke with both women, then led one off to dance.

"Good luck," she murmured. "It's not going to work."

Unfortunately as she spoke, the music faded and one of the sisters—Natalie, she would guess—flounced away.

"What is not going to work?" the king asked Maggie.

"I, ah—" She looked around frantically for a way to escape. "Ah, nothing."

"It is not nothing. It is important that all my sons marry. As they seem to be in no hurry to find a bride on their own, I am forced to interfere."

Maggie remembered what Victoria had said about the beheading and hoped the other woman had been kidding.

"You can't lead a woman to him like that," she said cautiously. "Not that your choices aren't lovely, lovely young women."

The king glared at her. "I assume you have a reason for saying that."

"Because men like the chase." Jon had told her all about it several times. They'd laughed about his friends and their disastrous love lives, secure in the comfort of their own relationship. "Did you see the movie *Jurassic Park?*"

"No."

"You should rent it. Or have it delivered or something. Men are like the T-Rex. They don't want their next meal handed to them. They want to hunt it down. By meal I mean—"

"Women. Yes, I understand the analogy." He looked out at the couples dancing then turned back to her. "You're sure of this?"

"Sort of." At the moment she wasn't sure of anything except she really wanted to be done talking to the king.

"Who is he hunting now? You?"

"What? No. No. Not at all. I work for him."

The king frowned. "Doing what?"

"Restoring a car." She held out her hands to show him the scars and calluses. "See? I'm not anyone. Really."

"For not anyone, you're very free with your opinions. Come with me."

He started walking without once glancing back to see if she was keeping up with him. Maggie entertained a brief thought at ducking away, then she reminded herself she lived at the palace. Total escape was impossible and she really did want to keep her job.

The king stopped and motioned her forward.

"Do you know any of these people?" he asked.

She looked at the unfamiliar faces, then shook her head.

What followed was a rapid set of introductions to people she'd only read about in the newspaper, including two American senators, a impossibly thin starlet and the Russian ambassador to El Deharia.

Maggie murmured greetings and tried to ignore the fact that she was barefoot. Thank God her gown trailed onto the floor and no one could see. Still, she couldn't help covering one foot with the other, as if to hide the truth.

Conversation flowed for a few minutes, ranging from a recent Grand Prix time trial to the continuing rise in oil prices. Maggie kept her mouth firmly closed and wished for someone to rescue her. Unfortunately she was on her own.

Then the Russian ambassador, a handsome older man, smiled at her. "May I have this dance, Miss Collins?"

Everyone looked at her. Maggie did her best not to blush. "Thank you, sir. It would be a pleasure."

At least she hoped it would be. If he danced as well as Qadir, she wouldn't have a problem.

He took her hand and led her to the dance floor. The music began and they were moving together. It wasn't as easy as it had been with Qadir, and not nearly as exciting, but she didn't step on him or stumble.

"You are friends with the king?" he asked.

"We've just met."

"So you are not his mistress?"

Maggie did stumble over that. She steadied herself. "No." The next word should have been *ick* but that wasn't appropriate. "I work here, at the palace, Mr. Ambassador."

"I see. You may call me Vlad."

Did she have to?

"I am a powerful man, Maggie. We could be good for each other."

Her shock must have showed because he chuckled. "You are surprised by my honesty?"

Not exactly, she thought. Was it just her or was the whole thing really tacky?

"Mr. Ambassador—"

"Vlad."

She ignored that. "Mr. Ambassador, I'm afraid you have the wrong idea about me."

She had plenty more she wanted to say, but just then Qadir appeared at her side. "Maggie. There you are. Our dance is next." He smiled at the Russian. "Do you mind if I cut in?"

Vlad stepped back. "Of course not."

Qadir drew her against him. "What happened?"

"Nothing."

He waited. She sighed. "I think he was coming on to me. I'm not sure."

"He was."

"Yuck."

Qadir laughed. "He would not be flattered by your reaction."

"I barely know the man."

"He is powerful. For many women that is enough."

Then those women needed to get a life, she thought. "I didn't know what to say."

"You can start with no. That usually works."

"I'll remember that." Not that she was likely to run into any more ambassadors. "How was your dance with Sabrina?"

Qadir's gaze narrowed. "Are you mocking me?"

"Maybe a little. But she is a known breeder."

He moved them off the dance floor and out onto a balcony. The stone floor was cool on her bare feet.

"For you this situation is amusing," he grumbled. "For me it is anything but. I do not want an arranged marriage to a sensible young woman from a good family."

"Then what *do* you want?"

Qadir didn't answer. Was it that he didn't know or was he simply not prepared to share his private thoughts with her?

"Can the king force you into marriage?" she asked instead.

"No. But he can be difficult."

"He cares about you and it's not totally crazy that he wants his sons married. I'm sure he's more than ready for grandchildren."

"You're taking his side?" Qadir asked.

"No. I'm pointing out that while his tactics are a little obvious, he means well. He cares, which should be worth something."

"If he were to turn his considerable interest on getting *you* married, I suspect you would change your mind."

"Maybe," she murmured thinking she wouldn't mind a little meddling from her own father. It would mean he was still around to bug her. Right now that sounded lovely.

"So he wants a good breeder," she said, "and you want to fall in love?"

"Love is not required. I would settle for mutual respect and shared interests."

Neither sounded very romantic, Maggie thought, but then

she wasn't royal. She wanted a lot more than that. Passion, excitement. She wanted to be swept away. She wanted a deep love that would last forever.

Qadir walked around the edge of the dance floor, both watching Maggie dance with his cousin and avoiding Sabrina, Natalie and any other woman of whom his father would approve.

Nadim danced with Maggie as he did everything in his life—with great competence and little real interest.

Nadim was sensible. In truth he lacked personality. Even as a child, Nadim had been boring.

Qadir, As'ad and Kateb had been close, always getting into trouble together, playing tricks on unsuspecting palace staff and causing their father to constantly threaten them with banishment. Nadim had always followed the rules.

Even now, as the song ended, Nadim bowed politely to Maggie, then turned away, never once noticing her bare feet or the way she adjusted her dress to make sure no one caught sight of her toes.

His gaze shifted to the left where he saw Natalie—or was it Sabrina?—glancing around the room as if searching for someone. He moved deeper into the crowd.

While he was pleased his brother As'ad was celebrating his engagement to Kayleen, Qadir wished only for the ball to be over. If he had to meet one more "appropriate" young woman, he would ride into the desert and join his brother Kateb, living in the villages, far from the palace.

It wasn't that he objected to marriage…at least not in theory. But practice was a different matter. While he wasn't waiting for the fantasy of falling in love, he wanted to feel *something* when he chose his future wife. Anticipation would be good. Pleasure.

Even a comfortable level of fondness. So far, he hadn't felt anything.

He'd been in love once, he reminded himself, and once had been enough. He wasn't interested in love, as he'd told Maggie, but he insisted on something more than simple disinterest in a marriage of convenience.

He saw As'ad bend down and say something to Kayleen. They looked happy. Not only had his brother found the right woman, but he'd managed to get their father off his back. If only Qadir could do that, as well.

What he needed was an engagement, he told himself. Or at the very least, a serious relationship. While he knew dozens of women who would be interested, he found himself not the least bit intrigued by any of them. One of life's ironies, he supposed.

He saw Maggie move toward the buffet. She ignored the caviar and went right for the tiny quiches. She popped one in her mouth, then licked her fingers.

The action was quick and unstudied, yet he found it erotic. The flick of her tongue against her skin made him think of doing the same to her himself. All over.

The heat that accompanied the thought was nearly as surprising as the image now planted in his brain. Maggie? Sexy?

She was competent and he enjoyed speaking with her. He liked teasing her and the sound of her laugh, but nothing more. She worked for him. She wasn't the type of woman who played his kind of game. She was…

Perfect, he thought as he studied her. Sensible, hardworking and not the least bit pretentious. While she hadn't come out and said money was an issue in her life, he knew she'd wanted the job because of the high fee involved. Was she willing to sell other services that might help him distract his father?

* * *

"It's almost like Christmas," Maggie breathed as she stared at the stack of boxes waiting right outside her office. She'd arrived a little late this morning. The party had gone on long into the night and she'd stayed far later than she'd expected. It had made getting up with her alarm a bit of a challenge. But now that she was here, she stared at the packages and forgot to be tired.

She wasn't sure where to start, she thought happily as she dug through her desk for a utility knife to slit open the first box. There were so many choices, so many possibilities.

"You look happy."

She turned and saw Qadir walking toward her. While the tux was gone, he still looked pretty darned good in his tailored suit.

"I love fast delivery," she said, pointing to all the boxes. "It's like a miracle. I don't know where to start. There are so many possibilities. Headlights, gears, pistons, brackets."

He stared at her for a long time. "You're a very unusual woman."

"I know. I've heard that before." She found the utility knife and moved toward the first box. It was small and light. The possibilities were endless!

She pressed the knife to the seam, then looked at him. "You want to open the first one?"

"Not especially."

"Okay." She slit the tape, then dug into the box. She pulled out the clear plastic bag within. "O-rings. Aren't they beautiful?"

Qadir laughed. "As I said—unusual. I would like to speak to you for a moment, Maggie."

"Okay."

She put the O-rings back in the box and followed Qadir into her office, where she settled on the corner of her desk and looked at him.

She told herself it was silly to be nervous. She hadn't done much on the car yet so it was unlikely he was upset about anything. Not that he looked upset. His expression was as unreadable as ever, although not in a hostile way. He looked very…princelike. And handsome, she thought absently, liking the firm set of his jaw and the way his eyes seemed to see so much more than they should.

"What do you think of me?" he asked.

The unexpected question made her blink. "Um, what?"

"We get along, do we not?"

Was that a trick question? "Yes."

"Good. I agree."

With what? What were they talking about?

"We have much in common," he continued.

That nearly made her laugh. What did they have in common? A love of fine Arabian horses? Jetsetting around the world? Hardly.

"Cars," he added. "We both like cars."

"Okay," she said slowly. "Sure. Cars."

"I mention this because I was thinking about your business back home."

The one she'd lost, she thought sadly. "It's not exactly what it was," she told him.

"The loss of your father would have changed things."

More than he knew. "It was hard while he was sick. He was in the hospital a lot and I was with him. It was hard to stay on top of things."

"Of course. When you return, you'll have more time."

She nodded, thinking she would also have a fair amount of money, although not enough to buy back the business. Still, she could start over with her own small shop. Continue the work.

"More money would help," he said.

"It usually does." A hopeful thought appeared. "You have a second car?"

"Not exactly."

"Then…"

"I have a proposition."

If she'd looked anything like Victoria, she would have assumed he was coming on to her. However, she stood there in coveralls that had been patched more than once, no makeup and her hair pulled back in an uneven ponytail.

"Which is?"

Qadir smiled. "You may have noticed my father's enthusiastic efforts to interest me in a woman. Any woman. He's determined to get all his sons married as quickly as possible."

"Typical father behavior," she said, then grinned. "Well, not counting the whole 'good breeder' part of the introduction."

"Exactly. I am not interested in being pressured. However, the only way to get my father to back off is to give him the impression I'm involved with someone and that it might be serious."

She nodded. "That would probably work."

"I'm glad you agree. So I propose an arrangement between us. We would date for a period of weeks. Perhaps three or four months, then say we are engaged. Nothing would be formally announced, of course, although there would be hints. Then a few weeks after that, we would have a heated argument, you would return to your country and I, heartbroken, couldn't possibly consider getting involved again for the rest of the year. Perhaps longer."

She opened her mouth, then closed it. His words had actually entered her brain—she knew she'd heard them. But they hadn't made any sense. He couldn't be saying what she thought he was saying.

"I… You… It's…"

He smiled. "A relationship of convenience," he said. "You will consent to be someone I become involved with for an agreed upon period of time—say, six months. I will, of course, pay you for your time."

He named an amount that made her already spinning head threaten to fall off and explode.

He wanted to fake *date?* Then get fake engaged to her? And *pay* her? All in an attempt to trick his father, the king?

"If he finds out about this, he'd kill me."

"Not in the traditional sense. He would be unhappy."

Not exactly comforting, Maggie thought. "Just go out with one of the women he introduces you to. Why won't that work?"

"None of them interest me."

"Sabrina seemed really nice."

He rolled his eyes. "You didn't have to dance with her."

"Lucky me." She stared at him. "You can't mean this."

"Why not? It's an arrangement that works for both of us. I don't have to deal with the king's matchmaking and you get to make extra money. I know the plan requires you to stay in El Deharia longer than you'd planned, but you will also earn a considerable sum for your trouble."

More than considerable, she thought, unable to take it all in.

"I'm not princess material," she said. "I work on cars."

"You are delightfully different."

If only. "I don't know how to dress or say the right things. You should ask Victoria. Nadim's secretary," she added when Qadir looked blank. "Pretty, blond, a great dresser."

"You and I get along. Spending time together would not be a hardship."

She thought of the dance they'd shared at the ball. Nope, not a hardship at all. Especially if there was more dancing. She wouldn't even object to kissing.

The image of them pressed together was so intense and so unexpected, she scrambled to the other side of the desk to put some distance between them.

"This is crazy," she said. "Let's all take a deep breath and start over."

"It isn't crazy. It's a sensible plan that benefits us both. I get peace and quiet for at least a year. You get to work on my car, then vacation in a beautiful palace, all the while getting paid. I will provide you with an appropriate wardrobe, a chance to meet world leaders. We will travel and attend conferences. In time, the relationship will end and you will return home with a much larger bank balance."

"It's a whole lot of trouble just to get your father off your back."

"You have never had to deal with a monarch as a parent."

Good point.

She was tempted. Not only by the money, but by the opportunity. When else could she have an experience like this? Plus, a teeny, tiny, shallow part of her, the part that was still ashamed of what had happened with Jon, sort of liked the idea of him thinking she was dating a handsome prince.

"We would need ground rules," she said.

"Such as?"

"You can't be going out with someone else while we're fake-dating. I don't want to be cheated on."

"Agreed. Although the same rules apply to you."

She smiled. "Not a big issue for me, but thanks for worrying." What else? "I don't want any of this in the papers. Do you guys have tabloids out here?" The idea of Jon knowing was one thing, but having a fake relationship played out in the media was another.

"We have some local coverage," he said. "It is nothing like what exists in America and Europe. I would want some minor mention of us dating to convince my father, but nothing more."

"Okay." She hesitated. "I feel like I should ask more, but I can't think of what it would be."

"You've dated before," he told her. "This will not be all that different."

Except for not falling in love with the guy.

She looked at Qadir. "Are you sure about this? You do remember I'm a car mechanic, right? I don't do the long-nail thing."

"Yes, I know and please, do not recommend your friend Victoria again. I thought of this last night at the ball. You did extremely well there. Remember, the Russian ambassador was interested."

"I don't think that's a very high bar," she said.

"Regardless, you're the one that I want. Yes or no, Maggie?"

Was she crazy to consider the offer? If she said yes, she would have enough money to buy three shops back home. She would be set for a long, long time. She would also not have to return to Aspen and watch Jon and Elaine fall deeper and deeper in love.

It wasn't as if there was any pressing reason to say no. She didn't have to be anywhere or do anything by a certain time. She was sadly free from commitment.

Maggie couldn't think of a single downside. She supposed there was the remote possibility of falling for Qadir, but honestly—what were the odds of that? He was nothing like Jon and Jon was the only man she'd ever been in love with. So she was perfectly safe.

She drew in a breath. "Yes."

"Excellent. We will meet again soon to work out the details."

"Fine."

"I will let you return to your packages."

He approached as he spoke. She straightened and started to lift her right hand so they could shake on the deal. Instead Qadir cupped her cheek, bent forward and brushed her mouth with his.

The touch was light, quick and not the least bit sexual. Still, when he stepped back she felt the burn all the way down to her toes. Something sharp and needy twisted in her stomach and made her want to lean into him so he could kiss her again and this time do it like he meant it.

Her reaction stunned her. She hoped she answered as he said goodbye, but she couldn't be sure. She could only try to breathe through the desperate need to have him kiss her again and know that she had just dropped herself into a level of trouble that she'd never been in before.

Chapter Five

Maggie spent the rest of the morning trying to figure out what she'd gotten herself into. Fake dating a sheik? That sort of thing didn't happen to anyone, let alone someone like her. Maybe Qadir had a brain disorder that left him confused. Maybe he'd been kidding. Maybe she'd imagined the whole conversation and the next time she saw him he would call her "Ms. Collins" and look right through her.

Rather than make herself crazy with all the possibilities, she opened packages, savored the thrill of her car parts, then started an inventory base. It was nearly one before she noticed she was starving. But before she could cross to the phone and order lunch, Qadir appeared with a folder in one hand and a picnic basket in the other.

"We have much to discuss," he told her. "Is now a convenient time?"

If it wasn't, did she really get to say so? "If you brought lunch, then now is fine," she told him.

"A conditional acceptance?"

"I'm starving."

"So you can be bought with food."

"Sometimes." Based on their deal, she could also be bought with money, but she didn't want to think about that.

They went into her office where she laid out the lunch he'd brought.

She eyed the white-chocolate macadamia-nut cookie and knew that if she had been alone, she so would have started with that. Next time, she told herself with a sigh, thinking one day she was going to have to go down to the kitchen, find whoever provided the daily baked cookies and give him or her a big hug.

"I had my assistant make a list of possible places and events for us to go to," Qadir said when she'd taken her first bite of the sandwich. "The choices are divided into events that are purely public and those that will be perceived as private."

Maggie nearly choked. "You told your assistant about our deal?"

"No. I asked for an updated social calendar. Then he prepared a list of restaurants where photographers were known to frequent. I'm sure he thinks we'll be avoiding those places."

She managed to swallow without killing herself. "Okay. That makes sense." They would have to be seen to convince people—meaning Qadir's father—that this was all real. "Is the king going to be upset about this? I'm nothing like Sabrina or Natalie."

Qadir smiled. "Which is a good thing."

"In your mind. What about in his?"

"He is not the one dating you."

She narrowed her gaze. "Be serious. I don't want the king hating me or ordering me out of the country because I'm not a known breeder."

"Don't worry about anything. My father will be delighted to think I am finally getting serious about someone. It has been a long time."

How long? Maggie remembered her first night at the palace when she'd overheard Qadir and the king talking about someone from Qadir's past.

He put the list on the desk between them. "I have marked several events I suggest we attend, but the others are discretionary."

She glanced from the paper to him. "I don't understand. You're saying I get a vote, too?"

"Of course. Why would you not?"

Because he was a royal and she wasn't. "Okay," she said slowly. "That's nice."

He smiled at her uncertainty. "You keep forgetting, I'm the most charming of all my brothers."

"So you say. I haven't actually talked to any of your brothers so I only have your word on this."

He grinned. "You'll have to trust me."

For reasons that weren't clear to her, her gaze dropped to his mouth. She found herself reliving that brief but powerful kiss they'd shared.

She'd reacted so strongly to the lightest of touches. It had been the strangest thing…most likely brought on by too much champagne—even though she couldn't remember having more than half a glass. Or maybe it had been because she hadn't eaten. Whatever the cause, it hadn't meant anything. Forgetting it had ever happened made the most sense. Except she couldn't seem to forget.

"Maggie? Did you want to make some suggestions?"

"What? Oh. Sure."

She glanced down at the neatly printed possibilities. There were plays, sporting events, a hospital wing opening. The shower for Kayleen and the wedding to follow were in bold.

"These are..." she asked.

"Required. The shower for you and the wedding for both of us."

If she'd been standing she would have backed up a couple of feet. "I can't go to Kayleen's wedding shower. I barely know her."

"If we are together, then you are part of the family."

"I don't want to lie to your family."

He leaned back in his chair. "Deception is the nature of our endeavor."

Most of the time he sounded like a regular guy, but every now and then he said something princelike.

"I've never been a very good liar," she admitted. "I'd hate to see that change."

He said nothing, as if giving her the time and space to change her mind. Did she want to go through with this?

She thought of her father fading away. He kept making her promise that after he was gone she would try to get the business back. He hated that his illness had caused them to lose everything. She'd never blamed him, never wished for anything except his recovery. She knew he would want her to have a financial cushion. He would probably find the whole situation with Qadir funny. Then he would squeeze her shoulder and tell her not to do anything he wouldn't do.

The memory made her both happy and sad. With her father gone, she was alone in the world. The deal with Qadir offered her a level of financial freedom she'd never experienced. She would be a fool to walk away.

"I've never been to a wedding shower," she told him. "I'm sure it will be fun."

"Excellent."

They discussed other possibilities. There was a car show in neighboring El Bahar. They both agreed that would be a good choice.

"Will you want to pick out the engagement ring?" he asked.

She stabbed her fork into the pasta salad and sighed. "I'd deliberately forgotten about that part of the deal. Do we have to get engaged?"

"If I am to be crushed by your leaving, then yes."

She tried to imagine him emotionally crushed, but her imagination failed her. Qadir was too strong and in charge.

"You know, you could make this a lot easier by just falling in love with some woman and getting married for real."

"I am aware of that."

"You shouldn't be so picky," she told him.

"Thank you for that extraordinary advice."

They returned to the list, but Maggie wasn't really paying attention. Once again she was remembering the mystery woman from Qadir's past—and wondering why it hadn't worked out.

Maggie stared at the clothes in her closet and wished desperately that she'd asked Victoria to help her get ready. She also wished she had at least a couple of nicer outfits. But dining with princes hadn't been on her weekly agenda in Aspen so her wardrobe tended toward supercasual with the odd somewhat less casual piece thrown in.

Her choices seemed to fall into two categories—long-sleeved T-shirts and short-sleeved T-shirts. She had a couple of blouses, one pair of black slacks and a ball gown that seemed as inappropriate for dinner as one of the T-shirts.

"I came here to work on cars, not date a sheik," she muttered as she flipped through the meager selection again, desperately hoping to see something she'd missed the first three times.

There was actually one other choice. A simple knit dress that she'd packed on a whim. It was burgundy, plain and a little too fitted for her taste. She'd bought it a couple of years ago when she'd wandered through a mall shortly after finding out her father had been diagnosed with cancer. It had been on sale. She'd tried it on as a distraction and then had purchased it because explaining why she didn't need it required too much effort.

Maggie wasn't sure why she'd tossed it in her suitcase. Fortunately the fabric traveled well.

She pulled off the tags, then brought the dress into the bathroom and started getting ready.

Once she'd showered and blown her hair dry, there wasn't all that much for her to do. She put on a little mascara, then lip gloss. Victoria had done a lot more to her the night of the ball, but Maggie had neither the skill nor the makeup. Qadir was going to have to suffer with her natural look.

She pulled on the dress, then stepped into a flat pair of sandals that weren't nearly as pretty as the ones she'd worn with her ball gown, but were a whole lot more comfortable. Then she glanced at the clock. It had taken her twelve minutes from stepping into the shower until she was ready to go. That included four minutes blow-drying her hair. Victoria would be horrified.

Thinking about her friend made her wonder what the other woman would think about the deal. Which made Maggie nervous. She put her hand to her stomach, as if that would help settle her nerves. Then someone knocked.

She opened the door to her suite and saw Qadir standing in the hallway. He looked as he always did—tall, handsome, well-dressed. Nothing was different. Except the tension in her stomach increased until she thought she might have to throw up. Just as intense was her need to have him pull her close and kiss her.

"Good evening," he said and smiled. "You are prompt. I should not be surprised."

"No, you shouldn't." She collected her purse and followed him into the hallway. "It doesn't take me long to get ready."

"And yet the result is lovely."

A compliment? She didn't know what to say. "Ah, thank you."

He chatted about something on the walk down to the front of the palace, but between her spinning head and swirling stomach, she had no idea what. When they entered the courtyard, a limo was waiting.

"I happen to know you have regular cars," she said as he held open the rear passenger door for her.

"Agreed, but this makes a better entrance."

Right. Because this was all for show.

She slid along the leather seat and tried to catch her breath. Fake dating, she reminded herself. Nothing more. She had no reason to be tense.

She forced herself to think calm thoughts. About ocean waves rushing in, then retreating. A cool, green forest. Water flowing in a brook.

"Maggie?"

She turned to him. "Yes?"

"What are you doing?"

"Trying not to throw up."

One corner of his mouth turned up. "You are always honest."

"I try to be."

"There is nothing to be nervous about."

"My stomach doesn't agree with you."

He shifted close and took her hand in his. "We are going to dinner at a very nice restaurant. You need to be calm so you can enjoy the meal. It is unlikely that we will be spotted by a photographer, however certain people will see us and that will start the gossip. Other than nodding politely to a few diners, little will be expected of you except eating."

"I'm a good eater."

"Then you will be fine."

His voice was so deep and low, she found herself getting lost in the sound. He rubbed her hand with slow, steady movements. That was nice, too, she thought as she felt herself relaxing.

This was just Qadir, she told herself. Just dinner. Nothing more.

She raised her gaze to his and found him watching her. With their eyes locked, he brought her hand to his mouth and kissed her palm.

It was a soft kiss that probably meant nothing. It was just…just…

Tension filled her stomach, but this was a whole new kind. It was hot and tight and had nothing to do with the rest of the world and everything to do with the man next to her.

Before she could figure out what she was supposed to do now, the car came to a stop. Talk about timing, she grumbled to herself.

The restaurant was on the water, with a beautiful view and the kind of low lighting that made everyone look good. They didn't have to wait, but were immediately led to a private table in an alcove.

"Thank you so much for joining us this evening, Prince Qadir," the hostess said, eyeing Maggie with obvious confusion. "I hope you enjoy your dinner."

The young woman nodded, then left.

Maggie shifted uncomfortably, wanting to explain that she wasn't *really* dating the prince. That the other woman didn't have to worry she would one day really be a princess. One thing for sure—she was going to have to talk to Victoria about going shopping in that secret back-room boutique. Better clothes were required for this whole fake-dating thing.

Still feeling out of place, Maggie picked up the leather-bound menu. As she did, she bumped one of the three different wine glasses set at her place. There was also a waterglass and an assortment of flatware, some of which she didn't recognize. Couldn't they have gone for a burger instead?

She opened the menu and stared at the pages and pages of choices.

"Do you have a preference for the wine?" Qadir asked. "French, Spanish, Italian? They also have an excellent selection from California, Washington, Australia and Chile."

"Whatever you would like is fine with me," she murmured, knowing she could never admit that the last time she'd had wine, it had been poured from a very lovely box purchased at Target.

She returned her attention to the menu, determined to pick something, but the words all blurred. She couldn't do this—she didn't belong here.

She looked up and found Qadir watching her.

"What's wrong?" he asked.

"Pretty much everything."

He surprised her by smiling. "If it is as awful as all that, then we have many areas where we can improve."

At least *he* found the situation amusing. "I'm not the right person for this," she whispered, leaning forward so he could hear her. "You've made a mistake."

"I have not." He took the menu from her hands and set it on top of his. "You are unfamiliar with the circumstances. This will get easier."

"I don't think so."

"Let me order for you. Do you have any food dislikes?"

This was a fancy restaurant. The possibilities for disaster were endless. "I'd just like something normal. Nothing squishy like sea urchin, or gross like paté."

"Very well. How about roast chicken with vegetables?"

"I could do that."

"Then that is what I will order."

A waiter appeared. He barely glanced at Maggie before bowing low to Qadir and thanking the prince for choosing the restaurant. A fast-paced conversation followed with wine chosen, entrées, salads and either appetizers or desserts picked. Maggie didn't recognize the names, so she couldn't be sure which.

The waiter left. Seconds later another man arrived with a bottle of white wine, along with a free-standing ice bucket. The wine was opened, tasted, pronounced excellent and poured. The second man left as quickly as the first.

"One can't complain about the service," Maggie murmured as Qadir lifted his glass. She took hold of hers and raised it, as well.

"To new beginnings," he said. "Let us give them a chance."

"A sneaky toast." Still, she touched her glass to his, then took a sip.

The wine was nice. Light and maybe crisp. She didn't really know the right terms. She knew she liked it and that she would probably faint if she knew how much it cost.

"Perhaps this will go more easily if we get to know each other better," he said, looking at her over his glass. "Tell me about your family."

"There's not much to tell," she admitted. "I'm an only child. My mom died when I was a baby. Dad always kept pictures of her around, but I don't remember her. It was just the two of us." She smiled. "I didn't mind. I couldn't miss what I'd never had and my father was great. He was one of the kindest men I've ever known. He took me with him everywhere, which is where I learned about cars. I grew up playing around them. I got in the way constantly, but then I learned how to help. It was a lot of fun. I learned math by helping with invoices. My dad made everything fun."

"He sounds like a good man."

"He was. He cared about people and loved his work. We lived

in a typical middle-class neighborhood. The houses were all the same and the kids played together. I was never into dolls or playing house. I was out with the boys. That was fine when I was young, but became a problem later. I didn't fit in either place."

She still remembered the horrible summer when she'd started to get curves. As minor as they were, they still made her feel as if she didn't fit in with the guys who had always been her friends.

"Feeling out of place made me hang out at the garage even more. It was the only place I felt comfortable."

She took another sip of wine. "Things got a little better in high school. I started seeing boys as something other than friends and they didn't seem to mind that I knew more about cars than they did. I never got really close to any of the girls, though."

She'd tried a few times, but hadn't known what to talk about. Makeup and clothes didn't interest her and she'd been too shy to admit to her crushes—a conversation point that might have allowed her to bond with the female half of the population.

"I would think the girls were jealous," Qadir said.

Maggie laughed. "I wish, but no. Then I started dating Jon. He lived next door. We'd been friends for years. One day I looked at him and everything was different. He asked me out and that was it. Being a couple allowed me to fit in. He was good to me. My dad liked him. We were together all through high school and while he went to college."

"Your relationship ended recently?"

"A few months ago."

Qadir studied her. "You are still in love with him." It wasn't a question.

"I'm not," Maggie said quickly, knowing it was true. "I miss him. He was my best friend forever. It was hard losing my dad, then Jon. I miss belonging and having someone to talk to. But I'm not in love with him."

Which made her behavior that night even more unforgivable.

Stop thinking about it, she told herself. Especially here, with Qadir.

Qadir didn't look convinced so she decided to change the subject. "What about your past?" she asked. "Yours must be more exciting, what with your being a prince and all. Don't women throw themselves at you wherever you go? Doesn't it get tricky, stepping over all those bodies?"

"It can be tiresome," he admitted, his eyes bright with humor.

She leaned toward him. "I want details."

"There aren't any of interest."

"No great love lurking in your past?" she asked before she remembered the mention of the mysterious woman the night she'd arrived.

Qadir picked up his wine, then put it down. "When I was very young—still in university—I met someone. Her name was Whitney."

"Was she from here?"

"England. I went to university there, although I did some graduate work in the States." He shrugged. "She was lovely. Smart, determined. She wanted to be a doctor. We fell in love. I brought her home to meet my father. I thought everything had gone well, but when we returned to England, she told me she couldn't marry me. She wasn't willing to give up her dreams to be my wife." He glanced at Maggie. "There are…restrictions that come with being a member of the royal family."

Made sense, she thought. "Whitney wouldn't have been able to practice medicine."

"Among other things. She's now in her final year of residency," he said. "She's a pediatric neurosurgeon."

Something that never would have happened if she'd married Qadir. "You still miss her."

"No. I respect her decision and I wish her well. It was a long time ago. We've both moved on."

Maggie was willing to believe he wasn't pining for Whitney. Qadir didn't seem the type to pine for anyone. But were there regrets?

Knowing about his past made him seem more like a regular guy, she thought. But was that a good thing or a bad one?

Qadir watched the play of emotions in Maggie's eyes. She was trying to put Whitney in context. Perhaps he should not have told her, but there was something about Maggie he trusted.

She wasn't like the usual women in his life. While she was certainly attractive, she lacked a sophistication he was used to. She didn't play games. And she knew more about cars than any female he'd met.

He started to tell her that when he saw a flash of movement out of the corner of his eye. He turned and saw a photographer easing along the far wall.

"An excellent opportunity," he said as he reached for Maggie's arm and pulled her toward him.

"What?"

Instead of answering, he kissed her. He had barely touched his mouth to hers when a flash went off. There was a flurry of activity as the restaurant staff raced for the photographer, no doubt to drag him outside. Qadir hoped they didn't take away his camera.

Even though the event had ended, Qadir continued the kiss. He liked the feel of Maggie's lips, the softness, the way she yielded. At times she was tough and in control, but now, she was all female—finding the true power of giving in.

He moved his hand to the back of her neck, where her long hair teased him. She smelled of soap and an elusive female essence that made him want to explore all of her. Need stirred.

He wanted to deepen the kiss. He wanted to taste her and

claim her and hold her. He wanted to feel her body next to his, even if all they did was kiss. But this was not the time or the place. Reluctantly he withdrew.

Maggie blinked several times. "Was there a flash?"

"I saw a photographer approaching. I wanted to give him something worthwhile."

She drew in a breath to steady her pinging nerves. "You did. Definitely."

The next morning Maggie had barely pulled on her robe when she heard someone pounding on her door. She walked through the living room of her suite and pulled open the door.

Victoria stood in the hallway, one hand on her hip, the other shaking a newspaper. "Do you know what's in here?" her friend said, pushing past her and walking into the room. "Do you have any idea?"

With that Victoria slapped the paper down on the dining room table.

There, in the middle, was a clear photograph of Qadir kissing a woman. At least she was pretty sure it was Qadir—his face wasn't visible. But hers was. Even with her eyes closed, she was easy to recognize.

Victoria crossed her arms over her chest. "There has to be a heck of a story because the last time you and I talked, you were barely calling the prince by his first name."

Maggie walked over to the coffeepot and turned it on. "It's not what you think."

"I don't know what *to* think."

While she and Qadir hadn't actually discussed keeping their deal quiet, it was certainly part of the bargain. But Victoria was her only friend in El Deharia and Maggie had a feeling she was going to need to talk things over with someone.

She turned. "Qadir doesn't want his father constantly bothering him with appropriate women, so he came up with a plan. I'm going to fake dating him for a couple of months, then we're going to get fake engaged. We'll have a big fight, I'll go home to Aspen and he'll go into mourning. That's all it is. A business proposition. He's paying me and to be honest, I can use the money."

Victoria stared at her. "Fake dating?"

"Uh-huh."

"Is it a lot of money?"

Maggie grinned. "Oh, yeah."

"Well, you go, girl."

"You're not mad?"

"No. I'm bitter. I should have thought of something like that for Nadim. At least then he would have to acknowledge I was alive. Fake dating, huh? You have to make him take you to some very cool places. He's a prince. He knows the global hot spots. You can…" Victoria swore under her breath. "Do you realize what this means?"

"What?"

"With the pressure off Qadir, the king is going to try to find Nadim a suitable bride. Knowing Nadim, he'll agree and that will be that."

Maggie poured them each a cup of coffee. "You aren't in love with him. Maybe you need to let the whole prince thing go."

"Maybe. It's just I'd be a really great princess."

Maggie noticed her friend sounded more resigned than heartbroken. Maybe a distraction would help.

"I desperately need your help," Maggie said. "Would you have time to go back to that consignment place? I have a fabulous wardrobe of T-shirts and nothing else. I don't want to embarrass him. Qadir is going to be taking me places other than the garage."

"Good point." Victoria stared at her for a long time. "Sure, we can go shopping, but I have a question first."

"Which is?"

"Are you sure about this? Have you thought it through?"

Maggie didn't understand the question. "Are you saying Qadir might not want to pay me the amount he's agreed to?"

"Not at all. I'm sure the money will be transferred with no problem. I was thinking more about not getting involved."

With Qadir?

Maggie immediately thought about their brief but powerful kiss. He made her quiver with the lightest touch. She told herself it was nothing more than chemistry and circumstances. She would be fine.

"It's a business deal."

"So it seems. Just remember that princes aren't like other men. Keep your heart safely protected."

Maggie laughed. Her body she could worry about but her heart was safely out of reach. She'd been hurt too much to ever give it again.

"Don't worry about me. I'll be fine."

Chapter Six

Qadir nodded to himself as he read the screen. All was well. Not that he expected less, but confirmation was always pleasant. He saved the information. His phone buzzed.

"Yes?"

"Sir, there is a Victoria McCallan to see you. She has no appointment but insists it's very important."

Qadir's male assistant didn't sound convinced of the fact. Qadir hesitated. Victoria was Nadim's secretary. Why would she need to come here? Still, the woman had never bothered him before. He could afford to give her a few minutes of his time.

"Send her in."

Seconds later an attractive blonde walked into his office. "Thank you for seeing me, Prince Qadir. I know you're busy."

He offered her a seat, but she shook her head. "I prefer to stand."

He rose, as well. Interesting. "How may I assist you?"

Victoria drew in a breath. She was visibly nervous, although she seemed to be trying to hide her upset.

"I want to talk to you about Maggie," she said. "I know about your deal."

Any natural instinct to aid turned cynical as he eyed the woman. Maggie had innocently shared the information of their deal with someone she perceived to be friend. Now Victoria sought to use that information for herself. Typical.

His brother Kateb was right—too many women were out for what they could get.

He waited for her to continue.

"Maggie isn't going to handle this well. She's not girly. She doesn't do the hair and makeup thing. She doesn't have the right clothes."

"But you do." He wasn't asking a question.

"What? Of course I do, but that's not the point. She's blunt and funny and sweet. She cares about people. Going out with you means getting mentioned in the papers. Maggie isn't going to like that."

Women didn't often confuse Qadir, but he now found himself at a loss. "You are concerned about your friend?"

Victoria's gaze narrowed. "Of course I care about my friend. Why else do you think I'm here?"

Her question hung in the air. He saw the exact moment she realized what he'd been thinking. Her back went stiff. Her mouth thinned.

He waited for her to start defending herself or even yelling at him. Instead she sucked in a breath and continued.

"My point is, Maggie is playing out of her league. You need to make sure she doesn't get trashed in the papers. And don't spring stuff on her. She's never done anything like this. She's going to have to figure it out while she goes. This is a tough time for her. She's dealt with a lot of loss in the past few months."

Victoria obviously knew about Maggie's father. He wondered if she knew about the old boyfriend.

As he listened to Victoria talk he realized he had never considered Maggie's feelings about the situation or how she would react to being thrown into his world. He'd seen her as someone he liked and enjoyed spending time with. He knew her to be honest, which made her the perfect candidate for his pretense. He should have considered whether his plan might hurt her in any way.

"She needs a makeover," Victoria said.

Qadir stared at her. "A what?"

"A makeover. Maggie's pretty, but she's the country mouse. She needs a new wardrobe. And someone to teach her how to wear makeup and do her hair. Maggie's proud and sweet. She doesn't deserve anyone asking why someone like you would bother with someone like her."

He didn't like Victoria saying that. "No one who knew Maggie would ask that question."

"I agree, but we're not going to be dealing with people who know her, are we?"

As much as he hated to admit it, she had a point. "I will see to it."

"Good. Look on the bright side. How often do you get to meet a beautiful woman who has no idea how great she is?"

Victoria was right, although he found himself hoping Maggie didn't change too much through the process.

"There's one other thing," Victoria said as the nervousness returned.

He waited.

She raised her chin. "You can't hurt her. She doesn't deserve that. You can't use your position or power against her."

Annoyance filled him. "You challenge my integrity?"

"Among other things."

"I am Prince Qadir of El Deharia. No one questions me."

"Then this is going to be a bad day for you."

"I can have you deported."

"I don't doubt that. Maggie is my friend and I don't want you to hurt her."

She trembled. He could see it. Yet she didn't back down. She faced him, knowing she could lose her job and be sent home in disgrace.

His opinion of both women increased favorably. Victoria for being so willing to protect her friend and Maggie for inspiring such loyalty.

He wondered if Nadim had ever noticed the firebrand lurking behind Victoria's blue eyes. It was his cousin's loss if he had not.

Qadir walked around the desk and touched Victoria's shoulder. "I will not hurt your friend. Maggie is doing me a favor. I have no intention of making her regret her decision to help. We have a business arrangement. Nothing more."

Victoria shook her head. "That's what she said. It always starts out sounding so sensible, right up until someone gets hurt."

"But I don't want to," Maggie said, a distinct whine in her voice. "I don't like shopping."

Qadir laughed. "You are the first woman to ever say so."

"I'm sure there are other women who don't like to shop," she muttered, wondering if she could fling herself out the limo's rear door and survive the impact. She would probably end up with a few scars but they would be better than an afternoon spent shopping. She shuddered at the thought.

"If you are to spend time with me, you need an appropriate

wardrobe," he told her. "You came prepared to work on cars, not date a prince."

She knew he was right. She didn't have any clothes to wear to all the events he'd mentioned. She needed a decent wardrobe to be able to fit in. But shopping?

"Can't we use the Internet?"

"No."

"We could send them my measurements. Wouldn't that work?"

"No."

"But there—"

"No."

She slumped back in her seat. "This really sucks."

He laughed.

They pulled up in front of the exclusive boutique where she and Victoria had come before. Maggie had a feeling they weren't going to be checking out the consignment room.

"Not here," she told him. "It's too expensive."

He turned to her. "Maggie, do you know how much I'm worth?"

Not even a clue. "A lot?"

"Exactly."

She eyed the store. She didn't want to go in, but then she didn't want to go to any store. "Okay, but they offer a palace discount. Make sure you use it."

He was still laughing when they walked inside.

Last time she'd been here, she and Victoria had moved through the large boutique without being acknowledged by a single assistant. Now it seemed as if every employee descended.

"Prince Qadir, you are here. How lovely to see you."

"Prince Qadir, as always you brighten our day."

"How may we help you?"

"What can I show you?"

Maggie slipped behind him for protection.

Then a tall, elegant woman of indeterminate age glided toward him.

"Prince Qadir," she said in a low, cultured voice. "You honor us with your presence."

"Thank you, Ava." He turned to Maggie. "This is Ava. She owns the store. She'll be helping us today."

Ava smiled at Maggie and took her hand. "Welcome, my dear."

Maggie wanted to slink away. Ava was one of those perfect women who looked like she would never wear anything that didn't match or had a stain or was sensible.

"Maggie is very special to me," Qadir said. "But not much of a shopper. She needs a complete wardrobe. One that prepares her for anything. However, I will warn you—she will resist this process. I'm counting on you to convince her all is necessary."

Ava smiled at Maggie. "My pleasure. Come, child. We have much to do. Let's get started."

Maggie felt like the fly being led away by the spider. She wanted to yell back at Qadir not to leave her alone with this woman, but she knew he wouldn't take her seriously. He thought this was funny. Which was just like a man. Someone should pinch and poke him while forcing him to wear stupid clothes. Then they'd see how much *he* liked it.

Ava led her to a large dressing room where they both stood in front of the three-way mirror. Maggie looked and felt frumpy next to the other woman. She sighed.

"What would you say your style is?" Ava asked.

"I have no idea."

"Casual, I'm thinking. You're not the sort of person to ever really enjoy wearing a dress." She turned Maggie so she was facing the mirror sideways. "Hmm. You have a perfectly good figure, but those jeans do nothing for you. I have a couple of styles in mind that will make you look spectacular."

Maggie stared at her. "Jeans?"

Ava smiled. "Very expensive designer jeans, child. With the right accessories, a beautiful blouse and jacket, jeans can be worn many places. A casual dinner, a luncheon. Nothing with the king, of course."

Ava walked around her. "While I would normally want to put one of Qadir's young women in pretty dresses, that won't do for you. You'll just be uncomfortable. We'll do pants as much as we can, then separates. You're going to be stuck with dresses for evening wear, of course. There's no getting around it."

Maggie thought of the ball gown she'd worn and how it had made her feel. "Sometimes a dress is okay."

"I'm glad you think so."

"I can really wear jeans?"

Ava smiled. "I promise."

It was kind of funny how at that moment Ava transformed from a spider into someone really, really nice.

Three hours and Maggie wasn't sure how many outfits later, she found herself sitting in front of a mirror at a very upscale beauty salon. She knew the place had to be pricey because they'd offered her a latte, bottled water or cocktail before discussing her hair. No one had *ever* offered her a cocktail before cutting her hair. Of course the way her stomach was jumping, getting tipsy didn't seem like such a bad idea.

"Not too short," Qadir said as he stood behind the chair, next to the stylist—a short man with a ponytail. "I like her hair long."

"I agree." The stylist, whose name Maggie couldn't remember, ran his hands through her hair. "She has a natural wave. I want to layer it so we can see the movement."

Maggie wrinkled her nose. "Does anyone care that I hate my

natural wave?" It was one of the reasons she wore her hair as long as she did and always tied it back. To hide the natural wave.

"Not really," Qadir said with a smile, then bent down and kissed the side of her neck.

"But it's *my* hair," she murmured without much energy. She was too caught up in the tingles racing through her body.

It had been a nothing kind of kiss—the only kind Qadir seemed to give her. A light brush, a meaningless peck. Kisses for show. Kisses that stole her breath away and made her want to…to…to *something*. Kiss more. Kiss back. Beg. Instead she was forced to sit there quietly while they continued to discuss her hair.

In the end, they chose the layered style they'd talked about, along with subtle highlights.

"Could I be blond?" Maggie asked. "I'd like to be blond."

Qadir turned the chair so she was facing him. "You are beautiful just as you are."

Beautiful? He didn't mean that, did he? "But I'm getting highlights. Going blond is practically the same."

"Not to me."

"Should we have the whole 'this is my hair' conversation again?"

"I will not be listening."

He leaned in and kissed her. On the mouth. Firmly.

She told herself it was just so the people in the hair salon would gossip about them. She told herself it didn't matter to her at all, one way or the other. It was just a kiss.

But it felt like a lot more.

His lips were warm and firm, taking and offering at the same time. He braced himself on the arms of the chair so they weren't touching anywhere but their mouths. Still, that was enough to make her whole body sit up and take notice.

He moved his mouth back and forth before brushing her lower lip with his tongue.

Instinctively she parted for him. Anticipation made her tense. When he slid inside, she wanted to squirm closer, to take whatever he offered. Instead she lifted her hand to his shoulder and felt the strength of him.

His tongue touched hers. Sparks flew in every direction. He circled her as they began a dance so exciting, so erotic, she found it difficult to breathe.

She'd been kissed before hundreds of times. She'd made love. She'd experienced desire for a man. But nothing had prepared her for the hunger that consumed her whenever Qadir kissed her.

Wanting began low in her belly and spiraled out, filling every cell with a need that almost frightened her. She felt control slipping and worried she would beg him to take her right there, in the chair, in front of anyone who happened to be watching. She felt breathless and out of control. It was frightening…and yet she never wanted him to stop.

At last he pulled away. Something hot and bright burned in his dark eyes. She had a feeling he could see the same in her. Passion, she thought. Heady and unfamiliar, but more compelling than she'd ever thought possible.

"You are a surprise," he murmured.

"I could say the same about you. Of course it could be a prince thing. You might take special classes and be taught techniques not known to mortal man."

"I am mortal and there is no special training."

Which meant it was just him. A slightly scary thought.

"I must go. The car will return and the driver will wait to take you back to the palace."

"Okay."

"I look forward to seeing your transformation this evening."

"We're doing something tonight?" Not that she minded.

"A play."

"Right. You mentioned that. I should probably get a calendar."

"I'll have my assistant print out a schedule."

That made her smile. "I've never dated by schedule before. Maybe he should include suggestions on what I should wear. Formal, informal, strictly casual."

"If you like."

She started to say she'd been kidding, but then realized having that information would help. "Theater is dressy, right?"

"Yes."

"Okay." She thought about the clothes they'd bought earlier that afternoon. "I have a couple of things I can wear. What's the play?"

"A musical. *Les Miserables.* The king's favorite."

"Has he seen it?"

"Many times. He'll see it again tonight."

"Oh. He's going, too?"

"We'll be in his box. It will be a good opportunity for him to get to know you better. As the woman I'm dating."

With that he straightened and walked away.

The stylist returned. "He's so hot. You're really lucky. Are you all right?"

Maggie shook her head. The king was going to be there tonight? In the same box? Was she expected to talk to him?

Stupid question, she told herself. She would have to carry on a conversation and pretend to be Qadir's girlfriend and what if the king asked about her being good breeding stock? How was she supposed to answer?

"I think I'm going to be sick," she whispered.

"I get that a lot," the stylist said as he wheeled a cart close and reached for scissors. "Deep breaths. You'll be fine."

"I can't do this," Maggie said as the limo pulled up in front of the entrance to a very large, very old building. "I can't breathe,

I can't think. This was all a mistake. If I'd already accepted money, I would return it. Seriously, pick someone else. Fainting will not make the king like me."

"You're exaggerating your condition," Qadir said, not sounding the least bit sympathetic. "You said you like musicals."

She glared at him. "What does that have to do with anything? I can't meet the king."

"You already have."

"As a nobody. You're being deliberately difficult and for the record, I don't like it."

He laughed. He actually laughed.

"You'll be fine," he said as he stepped out of the limo and held out his hand to assist her.

"It's all fun and games now," she muttered as she followed him. "Let's see how amusing this is when I throw up on your expensive handmade shoes."

He had the nerve to chuckle again, then he tucked her hand into the crook of his arm and led her into the theater.

Maggie concentrated on walking in new shoes and breathing and trying not to think about the way her stomach flopped over and over and over. Look at the architecture, she told herself. Admire the clean lines, the soaring ceilings, the whatever the sticky-out parts were called by the corners.

Actually, now that she was paying attention, she realized the building *was* beautiful. Elegant and oddly feminine, if such an imposing building could be called that. There were mosaics and huge chandeliers, gilded pillars and archways. A staircase that seemed to glide up to heaven.

"What is this place?" she asked.

Instead of answering, Qadir came to a stop and turned her to her right. She stared at the handsome couple in front of them, then gasped when she realized it was them.

The large mirror showed her Qadir was as good-looking as always. Strong, tall and elegant in a tailored tux. The woman next to him wasn't half-bad, either, and the most amazing part was it was her.

The haircut had brought out the waves she hated, but somehow now they didn't look so geeky. Instead they were almost loose curls flowing to her shoulders. The makeup she'd been shown how to use made her eyes larger and mouth bigger. But it was the clothes she really liked.

True to her word, Ava hadn't tried to stick her in a dress. Instead Maggie wore white silk trousers and a white silk tank top. What transformed the outfit from day to night wasn't just the beading on the tank top, but the fact that her trousers were actually slit from ankle to thigh. While she was standing still, they looked perfectly conservative, but when she moved she flashed a whole lot of leg.

High heeled sandals made her even taller, although she was still several inches shorter than Qadir.

He put his hands on her shoulders. "You have nothing to be nervous about. You are beautiful, smart, funny and charming. The only problem we're going to have with the king is that he is going to want you for himself."

That made her smile. "I think you're safe."

For a second she thought he was going to kiss her again. There was something in his posture and the look in his eye. But then he took her hand and pulled her along toward the stairs.

Disappointment chased away the last of her nerves. She wouldn't have minded a little premusical kissing. Honestly, the way Qadir made her body go up in flames, she wouldn't mind a little anything with him. Something interesting to think about later.

They climbed the stairs and walked to the right. A guard stepped aside, allowing them to step into what Maggie assumed was a private box. She'd never been in one before.

There were several people standing around, drinking champagne and nibbling on appetizers. She had a sudden craving for those little hot dogs wrapped in pastry.

But before she could check out the food, the crowd parted and she found herself in front of King Mukhtar.

"Father," Qadir said, "I would like you to meet my date for the evening. Miss Maggie Collins. She's from America. Colorado."

Maggie tightened her grip on Qadir's fingers as she smiled at the king. "Your Highness, this is a great honor for me."

The king frowned. "Have we met?"

One of the guards came forward. "Your Highness, the photographers are here. Shall I let them in?"

The king nodded. Everyone shifted position as several men with cameras entered the booth and began snapping pictures. Maggie found herself blinded. Just when she thought she couldn't stand it anymore, the king waved his hand and the men instantly stopped.

"There's power," she murmured to Qadir. "It really is good to be the king."

"So I hear."

He gave her a glass of champagne. She took a sip.

"What am I supposed to say when he asks me what I do?"

"Tell him the truth," Qadir said.

Easy for him, she thought. He wasn't a car mechanic. "He's going to give me that look. The one that says I'm weird and that I should have gone for something more traditionally female."

"He's the king. He doesn't do looks."

"He'll have the look. Trust me."

Someone called Qadir away. Maggie eased into a corner and did her best to be invisible. She picked up a cracker with she wasn't sure what on top and had just taken a bite when the king walked over.

"This is your first time at our theater?" he asked.

She chewed quickly then swallowed. "Um, yes. Sir. The building is stunning. I was admiring it when we came in. There's something unique about the architecture." Or was there? She swallowed again but not because of any food. "At least it seemed that way to me."

"Early fifteenth century," the king told her. "One of my ancestors built this small palace for a favorite mistress. He promised to build her something as beautiful as herself. When it was completed she claimed that no woman could live up to such beauty. But she accepted the palace anyway."

Maggie grinned. "You have to respect a woman who enjoys real estate."

As soon as the words were out, she wanted to stuff them back in her mouth. There were probably a thousand different ways for someone to interpret that comment and most of them were bad.

But before she could think about throwing herself off the nearby balcony, Mukhtar laughed. "An excellent observation, my dear. Very funny."

She exhaled in relief. Time for a safer topic. "I'm looking forward to the performance tonight. I've heard most of the music from the show, but I've never seen it in person." She thought about mentioning she'd seen the performance on PBS, but maybe he wouldn't know what that was and she wasn't sure he would find the explanation interesting.

"You are in for an experience," the king said. "The music is compelling and touches one's soul."

Maggie didn't know what to say to that. Fortunately the lights flickered. Qadir returned to her side and guided her to their seats.

"I did okay," she whispered. "I didn't say anything stupid to the king."

Instead of answering, Qadir motioned to her right. She turned and saw Mukhtar sitting next to her.

She smiled tightly, then leaned to her left.

"You are so going to be punished for this later."

Qadir, of course, only laughed.

The orchestra began playing. At first Maggie was so aware of the king seated close, she couldn't relax. But eventually the story pulled her in. She found herself caught up in the events playing out on the spartan stage. When Javert killed himself, she felt tears in her eyes.

She did her best to blink them back, only to feel something soft pressing against her hand.

She looked down and saw a white handkerchief, then sniffed and looked at the man handing it to her.

"He was a good man facing an impossible choice," Qadir murmured. "His soul could only handle so much before it ripped in two."

She nodded without speaking, then wiped away her tears. He put his arm around her and pulled her close. She relaxed with his embrace, and felt safe for the first time in what seemed like forever.

Chapter Seven

Qadir stood by the office in the garage. It was his nature to take charge, to direct. Rather than give in to that need, he'd physically stepped back to let Maggie have control of the moment.

Gone was the sophisticated beauty from the previous night. Today she was all business, in coveralls and a T-shirt, her hair pulled back, her face scrubbed clean. She focused on nothing but the equipment and the men she directed as the engine was slowly lifted from the body of the Rolls.

Qadir knew he should be paying attention to the action. The engine was the heart of the car and if something happened to it then true restoration wasn't possible. Yet he couldn't seem to stop watching Maggie as she moved around the car, double-checking that everything was secure and then nodding for the men to resume.

There was something in the way she moved, he decided. Or

maybe it was knowing that she could be both this competent leader and yet feminine enough to cry because a character in a play died.

Her tears had startled him. He couldn't recall the last time he'd seen a woman cry for reasons other than manipulation. Later, as the musical had continued, Maggie had struggled for control, telling him or perhaps herself that she was fine.

"Swing it around," Maggie called out. "Slowly. We don't have any other plans for the day. That's it. Great job. Just like that."

He watched as the engine was lowered to the supports that would allow Maggie to work her magic on the aging beauty. When the engine was in place, Maggie breathed a sigh of relief and applauded her team.

"Excellent work," she told the men. "Thank you so much for your patience and attention to detail."

Qadir waited until everyone had gone to walk over to the engine.

"It could be worse," she told him without bothering to look at him. "I'll admit to a few moments of terror when it was pulled out. I thought there was more damage. But there doesn't seem to be any horrible surprises. It'll take me a few days to take everything apart and access the damage. That will really tell us where we stand."

She glanced up at him. "What? You're looking at me funny."

"You are an interesting combination of traits. You were very good with the men."

She rolled her eyes. "I've been working with men my whole life."

"These are men of my country, not yours. They do not usually take direction from a woman. Yet you established authority with them easily and offered them much praise. They will speak well of you."

"Don't be so surprised. I told you when you hired me, I know what I'm doing."

Surprise didn't describe his feelings. He was intrigued by her. Impressed. Aroused. But not surprised.

"The king likes you, as well," he said.

She pulled a rag from her back pocket and wiped her hands. "Okay, that one I don't know how to deal with."

"You should be pleased."

"Why? Wouldn't it be better if he didn't like me? We're going to break up. I don't want him mad at me when that happens."

Qadir smiled. "Fear not. I will keep him from locking you away when you break my heart."

"How comforting."

"You did very well at the theater. Our next event will be to have dinner with As'ad and Kayleen. That will be easier."

"Maybe for you," Maggie said with a sigh. "I'm not so sure. I only had to talk to the king for a couple of minutes. Dinner is a lot longer. They're going to ask questions like where we met."

"We met here," he reminded her.

"Oh. Right. Well, they'll want to know other stuff. Like what we see in each other."

A question he could easily answer, he thought as he watched her walk around the engine. Maggie was bright and funny and she spoke her mind. She was also a fascinating combination of competent and sexy. Like now. The coveralls hid everything, which only made him want to see and touch all that they concealed.

"My brother and his fiancée are within weeks of their wedding," he told her. "They have adopted three young girls. If the conversation turns too personal, ask about some detail in the planning or how the children are doing. I am confident that you'll be just fine."

"Wish I were." She walked over to the car and ran her hands along the side. "This I understand. This makes sense to me. Where art meets function. Couldn't I just stay here and work on the car?"

He crossed to her and touched her face. Her skin was soft, her eyes wide, her mouth…tempting.

"Do you wish to be released from our arrangement?" he asked, wanting her with a power that left him hungry and restless.

Her pupils dilated. "No. I just want to whine about it."

As always, she made him smile. "Then I will ignore your complaints."

"Fair enough."

"I must return to my office."

The need to kiss her was strong, but he resisted. He'd hired Maggie to convince his father he was involved. He would not take advantage of the situation, no matter how much she tempted him.

He left the garage and walked toward the palace. Halfway through the garden he realized he had not told Maggie what time they were to meet for dinner.

He retraced his steps. She wasn't in the garage, so he crossed to her office. The door was closed. He opened it without knocking and walked inside only to find Maggie changing her clothes.

She stood in the center of the room, her back to him. As he watched, the coveralls fell to the floor and she stepped out of them.

She'd already removed her boots, so she wore nothing but socks, tiny panties and a T-shirt.

Everything he'd been taught told him to retreat, to give her the privacy she expected and deserved. The blood of the desert that still pounded through his veins demanded that he take this beautiful, alluring woman.

He couldn't seem to look away from her long legs, the curve of her hip, the way she moved as she bent down to pick up the coveralls. She turned slightly, saw him and jumped.

Maggie was pretty sure she didn't scream, which was good because she hardly needed one more embarrassing moment where Qadir was concerned. Then she remembered she was kind of undressed and felt herself flush anyway.

"I...forgot to tell you what time we would meet for our dinner," he said.

"Isn't it seven? That's what my schedule says."

"Ah, yes. Seven."

She stood awkwardly, sort of holding the coveralls in front of her body, even as she tried to convince herself that panties and a T-shirt were more clothing than she wore to the beach. Only they weren't at the beach and she'd been undressing.

"I didn't mean to intrude," he said. "My apologies."

She appreciated the words, even as she noticed he wasn't leaving. That should have annoyed her. But there was something in the way Qadir looked at her that made her feel all shaky inside.

"Maggie." He crossed to her in three long strides. "Send me away and I will go."

His gaze was intense, as was his touch when he held her by her upper arms.

Sparks arced between them. She could practically see them as they singed her skin. Need grew until it devoured every part of her.

She didn't understand what it was about this man that made her react the way she did. Cosmic humor? Chemistry? Hormones? She didn't know and she wasn't sure she cared. She only knew that when she was close to Qadir, touching him, being touched, she felt more alive than she ever had in her life.

She dropped the coveralls. "That won't be necessary," she whispered.

He pulled her toward him with a force that caused her to lose her balance. Not that it mattered. She knew if she fell, he would catch her, just as he caught her now, pulling her against him, claiming her with a hot, wild kiss that threatened to steal her soul.

She leaned against him, her curves flattening against his hard chest, wrapped her arms around his neck and gave herself over to the kiss. She met him stroke for stroke. As he explored, she tightened her lips around his tongue and sucked. He stiffened.

Pleasure filled her, along with the confidence of knowing she wasn't the only one in danger of getting lost in the moment.

He dropped his hands to her hips then around to her rear, squeezing the curves, causing her to surge against him.

Her belly nestled against his arousal, hard, thick proof of what she did to him. Feeling it made her insides melt. She felt herself swelling in anticipation.

He ran his hands up and down her back before slipping one around her rib cage then up her T-shirt to her breast. Even through the layers of fabric, he found her nipple, tight and hard. He teased the sensitive point, rubbing it, circling, then brushing it with the palm of his hand.

At the same time he broke the kiss, only to nibble his way along her jaw.

He moved his free hand to her other breast. His touch was exquisite. Powerful need made her tremble. She wanted everything right that second. She wanted *him.*

He stepped back far enough to pull off her T-shirt. She quickly undid her bra and tossed it aside. Then his hands were on her bare skin.

He stroked her with his fingers before bending down and taking her nipple in his mouth. When he sucked, deep ribbons of desire wove their way down to that place between her thighs. She cupped his head with her hand, as much to be touching him as to make sure he never stopped.

His tongue danced with her, flicked against her, made her gasp and moan. Then he slipped one hand between her legs.

She braced herself for the magic of his touch and the intensity of her response. But even as he eased into place, she heard someone in the garage. A voice, then a burst of male laughter. She stiffened.

Qadir straightened. He immediately pulled off his suit jacket and covered her, then moved to the door, closed and locked it.

All that only took a second, but it was enough for her rational mind to wake up and be horrified by what had almost happened.

Qadir was her boss. They had a deal and that didn't include sex. Just as confusing was the fact that she'd never been the kind of woman who threw herself into bed with any guy who came along. There'd only ever been Jon and it had taken them three years of dating to finally go all the way.

Of course they'd been young and both virgins. Qadir was a man of the world. Which explained his actions, but what about hers? It was one thing to enjoy a man's kiss—it was another to get so swept away that she'd nearly done it in her office in the garage, in the middle of the day.

"Maggie?"

She looked at him. "I don't know what to say."

"I won't apologize."

He hadn't done anything wrong except take what was offered. "I don't expect you to."

"Would it help if you threw something?"

That made her smile. "I'm not sure. I don't feel angry. Just confused. I don't usually do this sort of thing."

"There is a powerful attraction between us."

"I got that."

He picked up her bra and T-shirt. After handing them to her, he turned his back. She set his jacket over a chair and quickly dressed. When she'd pulled on the coveralls, she said, "Doing anything…you know, intimate, would mess things up."

He faced her again. "I agree."

"I work for you."

He nodded. "Better to keep things business only."

"Yeah."

They were both saying the right words, so why did she have the feeling that neither of them believed them?

"You are all right?" he asked.

"Fine. Weirded out, but fine." She gave him a little push. "Go back to your office and do princely things. I'll be ready at seven."

"I'll be waiting," he told her and left.

Maggie watched him go. When she was alone, she sank into the chair and tried to figure out how much trouble she'd just gotten herself into.

Could she and Qadir put this behind them and pretend it had never happened?

Without meaning to, she closed her eyes and remembered how it felt to have his mouth on her breasts. Talk about amazing.

"It's just chemistry," she told herself. "Nothing more."

It couldn't be. She was here for a job and that was all. In six months their fake relationship would end and she would go home, much richer for the experience.

The trick was to not get personally involved. But for the first time she wondered if that was going to be harder than she'd ever imagined.

"Tell me about the woman," Kateb said as he shrugged out of his robes and tossed them over a chair in Qadir's suite.

Qadir poured them each a Scotch and handed his brother a glass. "What woman?"

Kateb raised his eyebrows. "Word of your involvement had even reached me in the desert, so there must be a woman."

They settled on the oversize sofas in the main living area. Qadir raised his glass in a toast to his brother. "It is good to have you back. You stay away too long."

"I find no pleasure in the city. I belong in the desert." Kateb took a sip of his drink. "But you have not answered my question."

"Her name is Maggie Collins. She's restoring the Rolls."

Kateb's expression gave nothing away. "And?"

"And she's beautiful, funny, down-to-earth."

"You say all the right things. What aren't you telling me, brother?"

Qadir grinned. "That it's a game. I'm paying her to pretend to be my girlfriend. In a few weeks, we'll get engaged. Then this will all be too much for her and she'll return home. Heartbroken, I won't be able to consider any of our father's offers for perhaps as long as a year."

Kateb nodded slowly. "An impressive plan."

"You wish you'd thought of it yourself."

"The idea has merit, although living in the desert as I do, I am well out of the king's reach."

"Lucky you."

Kateb took another drink. "You do realize the game may have consequences."

Qadir thought about his encounter with Maggie that morning, in the garage. If those were the consequences his brother was talking about, he would welcome them.

She had been all sweet fire in his arms. Her body yielding, her moans telling him she was as aroused as he had been.

"I am not concerned," Qadir told him. "I know what I'm doing."

"As you wish."

"Are you here to discuss the nomination?" Qadir asked.

Kateb shrugged. "I am not sure there is anything to discuss."

"They will name you and then what? Our father will not be pleased."

"I have never been able to please him."

"If you accept, you face him as an equal."

Kateb smiled. "The king will not see things that way."

Years ago, Qadir and his brothers had been sent into the desert, as was tradition. Young royal sons were taught the old ways, living with the nomads who roamed the deserts of the area. Qadir had endured the time but Kateb had loved it. As soon as he had finished university, he had chosen to make his home in the desert.

Tradition stated that every twenty-five years a new leader was nominated. As Kateb had become one of them, he was expected to be named.

But he was already an heir to Mukhtar's throne. Not the first in line, but still close to being king. For Kateb to accept the nomination of the desert people meant abdicating his rights to the El Deharian throne.

"What do you want?" Qadir asked.

"To stay where I belong. I am unlikely to be king here. Walking away from what will never be mine is not a hardship."

But if it was so easy, wouldn't Kateb have already made the decision?

"Apparently the kind of flowers matter," Kayleen said with a sigh. "There are rules."

"Ignore the rules," Prince As'ad told her. "You are to be my bride. Do what makes you happy."

"So imperious," Kayleen said, although she smiled at her fiancé. "It's easy for him to tell me to break the rules, but he doesn't have to face the wedding planner." She leaned toward Maggie, her eyes wide. "Do you know the president of the United States has been invited? I nearly passed out when they told me. Fortunately he can't come. They'll send someone else, which is great. I couldn't help fainting if I knew the president was there."

As'ad touched her cheek. "You are far too strong to faint."

"Maybe, but I'll sure be thinking about it." Kayleen shook her head. "I'm sorry. Hearing all this talk about the wedding must be really boring for you." She smiled. "Qadir especially."

"You are so lovely that any topic is interesting," Qadir told her.

Maggie had to press her lips together to keep from laughing. As'ad glared at his brother.

"Do not use your charm on my fiancée or you will suffer the consequences."

Qadir only looked amused. "Are you so unsure of her affections?"

Kayleen rolled her eyes. "They get like this from time to time. Sort of a royal way of letting off steam. We can pretty much send it in any direction we want. You could get insulted that Qadir is pretending to make a play for me or I could be flattered he thinks I'm worthy or we would ignore them altogether and just talk about something else."

Maggie had been nervous about the dinner with As'ad and Kayleen. She didn't know either of them and an intimate setting would require a lot of conversation. She had wondered how it would be possible to keep her fake relationship with Qadir seeming real.

But she found herself enjoying the evening very much. The other couple was easy to talk to. Kayleen especially bubbled about the wedding. They hadn't asked any awkward questions and seemed to totally accept her. Life being what it was, that made her feel a little guilty.

"Let's ignore them," Maggie said. "Tell me about your three girls. That's a lot to take on when you're just getting married."

"I know," Kayleen said, sounding totally thrilled. "But the girls are the reason As'ad and I are together. He adopted them—

it's a long, complicated story. Anyway, I was their nanny and we sort of, well…"

"Fell in love," Maggie said, seeing the truth in her eyes.

"Yes. It was wonderful. *He's* wonderful."

Maggie watched Kayleen look at her fiancé. There was so much love between them. So much caring. She felt a flicker of envy deep inside. A strong desire to have the same for herself.

She tried to remember if she'd ever felt that kind of connection before. Had it existed with Jon? She realized she wasn't sure. That their love had evolved slowly. How much of it had been proximity? Had they fallen in love because they'd both been together all the time?

She didn't have an answer, but as she considered the question she realized she wasn't sad. That thinking about Jon didn't depress her anymore.

She probed more deliberately. Didn't she miss him? Didn't she want them to get back together?

The answer came quickly. No. She still liked him and admired him, but the longing was gone. Even the simple need to talk to him burned much more quietly.

She still felt regret for that last night together. She wasn't sure how long it would take for the shame to ease. But except for that, she felt ready to put Jon behind her. She found herself genuinely happy that he'd found someone else and longed to do the same herself.

Involuntarily she found herself looking at Qadir. Was he the one?

That made her smile. Yes, the man was amazing and apparently had a direct and sexual line to her nervous system, but that didn't mean they would have any kind of serious relationship. Ever. The prince and the car mechanic? Not likely.

"Qadir is very nice," Kayleen said, her voice soft.

Maggie smiled. "He is. Not nearly as imperious as I would have imagined a prince to be."

"I think he's more low-key than the other brothers. Now Kateb is superintense. Have you met him?"

"No."

"He lives in the desert. He just got back. I talked to him for a few minutes earlier today. Wow. Talk about dark and dangerous. I kept wanting to hide behind As'ad."

"Why?"

"I can't really explain it. There's something about him that isn't completely…tamed. Hmm, that's the wrong word, but its the best one I can come up with."

An untamed prince?

"The king is already asking about grandchildren," As'ad said to Qadir.

Kayleen squeezed his hand. "But that's the fun part."

As'ad smiled at her. "You are too understanding. The king goes too far. We are not yet married."

"You could just tell him we're planning on having children fairly quickly. That would make him feel better."

"I will not give him the satisfaction."

Kayleen looked at Maggie. "See what I mean? Totally stubborn. How am I supposed to fight against that?"

"You are not," As'ad told her. He looked at his brother. "You know, if your relationship gets serious, he will do the same to you. The man is never satisfied."

Qadir reached for her hand. "Don't get scared. I'll protect you from the king."

"I'm not worried," Maggie told him. There was no way she and Qadir would ever be having the children discussion. She was here for a limited period of time. Sort of like the traveling theater. Not that she wouldn't want children one day.

She and Jon had always assumed they would get married and have kids. They'd argued about the number. He wanted three. She kept pointing out that practically, an even number was better. Then he joked about eight and they would laugh.

Instinctively she braced herself for the pain from the memories, but there wasn't any. She had truly moved on.

"It's kind of funny to have to worry about not getting pregnant early," Kayleen said. "Obviously one doesn't want to be a pregnant bride under any circumstances, but when the groom is a prince, it's a huge deal."

"It would only take one mistake," Qadir said cheerfully. "No pressure, brother."

As'ad growled some reply but Maggie wasn't listening. She found herself oddly frozen in time, as if she'd left her body and could see the party happening below her but wasn't a part of it anymore.

"No, no, no," she told herself silently. It wasn't that. It couldn't be. It had only been the one time. Off the pill, her period was never regular, so she wasn't technically late.

Fear clutched her, leaving her chilled to the bone.

One time with Jon. That single night.

As they had only ever been with each other, their only worry for protection had been pregnancy. She'd gone on the pill early in their relationship and all had been well. But after the breakup, she hadn't bothered, knowing she wasn't interested in being with anyone, at least not for a long time.

Which meant that she hadn't been taking birth control that last night she and Jon were together—and he hadn't used a condom.

"Maggie?" Qadir asked. "Are you all right?"

She nodded and tried to smile, even as she fought waves of panic. She couldn't be pregnant. Not now. Not with Jon's baby. That would be a massive disaster—one she wouldn't know how to fix.

* * *

After getting directions to the nearest couple of drugstores from Victoria, Maggie headed out first thing the next morning. She hadn't slept all night, even after telling herself that her period was late because of the stress she'd been through. One encounter did not a baby make. Or did it?

As her friend had promised, there were several shops on the street, with a drugstore at each end. Maggie went into the first one and prayed that El Deharia was a enough of a forward-thinking country that there would be pregnancy kits right there on the shelf.

She found the aisle with all the female products and breathed a sigh of relief when she saw the boxes that she had only previously seen on television. At least she wasn't going to have to ask the pharmacist.

She was about to grab one when she heard some odd whispering. She turned and saw a couple of teenage girls behind her. They were in school uniforms and carrying books.

"You're her, aren't you?" one of them said. "The girl dating Qadir. He's delicious. I like him the best. What's he really like?"

Maggie wondered if she was standing there with her mouth hanging open from shock. These girls had recognized her from those stupid tabloid pictures? Was it possible?

"Oh, hi," she said, feeling like an idiot. "He's really nice. Friendly."

"How did you meet?"

"I work at the palace."

The other girl sighed. "I wish I could get a job there. My mom says I'm not the type to do real work, but I could do something."

Her friend smiled. "He's the best. You're so lucky. Come on. We need to get to school."

They waved and left. Maggie walked around to the next aisle, where she picked up some bandages she didn't need. When she was sure the girls were gone, she returned to the first aisle and bought three different pregnancy kits. Then she went to the front of the store and paid for them.

What she didn't see was the third teenage girl lurking behind, her cell phone held high, camera at the ready. As Maggie fished money out of her wallet, the third girl started snapping pictures.

Twenty-four hours later, Maggie sat on her sofa trying to decide which was worse—the fact that she was pregnant, or the picture in the paper showing her buying the pregnancy kits.

And the speculation that the child was Qadir's.

Chapter Eight

Maggie couldn't believe it. There was her picture and she was clearly holding the pregnancy kits. Who had done that and how? Who walked around with a camera all the…

A cell phone, she thought as she sank onto the sofa and held in a groan. Those girls. Was it possible?

She looked at the grainy picture and realized it was more than possible. It had happened.

She didn't know what to think, what to feel. Remembering that last night with Jon, she knew it had to have happened then. But why did she have to be pregnant? Now? Like this?

She covered her face with her hands, ashamed, embarrassed, confused. This couldn't be real. She was asleep and she would wake up and be grateful that—

Someone knocked on the door. She didn't want to answer, but knew she couldn't hide out in her suite forever. She would have to face Qadir. She winced, thinking about how all this was going to effect him. What must he think of her?

She stood and walked to the door, then sucked in a breath and pulled it open.

She'd been hoping for Victoria. Instead a handsome prince stood in her doorway.

"I see by your expression you've seen the morning paper," he said calmly. "May I come in?"

She stepped back, then closed the door behind him. Heat burned on her cheeks. She had no idea what to say. She'd never planned on getting pregnant in the first place, let alone drag him into the mess, with people assuming the child was his.

"I feel horrible," she said, knowing she should be the one to start the conversation. "I had no idea about this. You have to believe me."

"I do." He looked at her, his dark eyes unreadable. "Jon is the father?"

She nodded. "There was one time, a few weeks ago. I was feeling lost and alone and things just got out of hand." She pressed her lips together. Okay, not the whole truth, but she was afraid to have him think even less of her by explaining it all in detail.

"It wasn't supposed to happen," she said. "Not that, not the pregnancy. We don't love each other. He's with someone else and I've moved on." She was more sure of that by the day. "I can't believe I'm pregnant."

Qadir looked at her. "You've taken the test to be sure? There is no mistake?"

"I wish there was. I didn't just take one test, I took three of them. I'm pregnant."

She waited for a reaction. An immediate statement that their deal was over. Maybe even orders to leave the country. But when he said nothing, she didn't know what to think. Worse, she couldn't look at him.

Maybe he was waiting for her to just pack her things and go. Her previous life hadn't prepared her for a situation like this. Everything was awkward enough, but his royal status added a whole new level of embarrassment to the conversation.

"This creates a complication," he said at last.

Despite everything she smiled. "You do have a talent for understatement."

"Jon will not be expecting you to be pregnant."

"Probably not." She drew in a deep breath. Okay—fine. She could be the one to say it. "Look, I know why you're here. You want me to understand that with things being the way they are, our deal is off. I get that. In your situation, I'd feel exactly the same way. But I'd really like to finish the car. I can do a beautiful job and being pregnant isn't going to make me any less skilled. To be honest, I need the job. I don't have health insurance and once I start to show, no one is going to want to hire me."

She felt panic flaring inside of her but refused to give in to it. Under the circumstances, she felt slimy enough just begging for her job. If she had any pride—or money in the bank—she would simply walk away. If it was just her, she would. But she now had a baby to think of.

A baby?

She pressed her hand to her stomach. No way. There couldn't be life growing inside her. She couldn't sense it. She didn't feel any different. Shouldn't she have a maternal connection or at least a clue?

"Do you want to leave?" he asked.

"What? Of course not."

"I have not suggested you should go."

"But I'm pregnant."

He nodded. "And people will assume the child is mine. What does it say about me that I let you leave the country?"

Maggie sank onto the sofa. She hadn't thought about that. "You'll have to issue a statement or something. Tell them it's not your baby. Some kind of official denial. People will think badly of me rather than you." Which she hated, but how could they get around that?

"Who will believe the child isn't mine?" he asked. "We have been seen together."

"Only for a short time and the baby not being yours is the truth."

"Why would that matter?"

She opened her mouth, then closed it. Good point, she thought, feeling alone and confused. Since when was truth a priority when it came to gossip?

"I'll tell the truth," she said slowly, hating that she would be known as a slut in public. "That I was with someone else. You're off the hook."

"You don't want to do that," he told her. "You will not enjoy the attention."

"I agree, but what choice is there? You're not taking the blame for this. You can't be the bad guy. I'm responsible."

"I'm the prince."

"What does that have to do with anything?"

"None of this would have happened if I hadn't asked you to lie on my behalf. I'm the one who put you in the public eye."

"I went willingly." She'd sold her soul for money. Her father would be so disappointed with her.

Before she could give in to that blow, the door to her suite opened and King Mukhtar swept inside. He held the paper in one hand.

"Is it true?" he demanded, glaring first at Qadir, then at her. "You are pregnant?"

If Maggie had thought she would squeeze in, she would have crawled under the sofa. But before she could make an attempt, Qadir pulled her to her feet and stepped in front of her, as if offering protection.

"This is none of your business," he said coolly as he faced his father.

"It *is* my business," the king told him angrily. "Is she pregnant? If so, the child cannot be yours. Unless you were seeing her before and brought her here specifically to meet me. Which you should have told me. Qadir, I demand to know what's going on."

Maggie cringed. "Your Highness," she began, only to have Qadir shake his head.

"Is it your child?" the king asked his son. "If so, I insist you marry her immediately. I understand having the wedding *after* the child is born is very fashionable these days, but this is my palace. I will not have it so."

"The baby isn't Qadir's," she whispered, wishing she really could disappear into the floor. "I'm sorry."

Qadir pulled her next to him and put his arm around her. "Don't apologize. You are not at fault here. The blame is mine." He looked at his father. "I paraded Maggie in public. That's why the pictures were taken. It is my fault."

"But not your child."

Maggie stared at the king, trying to figure out what he was thinking. He sounded almost disappointed by the news. Had he been hoping he would have a grandchild at last?

"No, Father."

Mukhtar nodded. "Very well. Maggie, you will leave El Deharia at once."

Maggie started to nod only to have Qadir say, "No, she will not. She's staying here."

"To what end? You can find someone else to work on your car."

"This isn't about the car. This is about her."

Maggie couldn't believe it. After all this, Qadir was still going forward with the deal? Didn't he know what a disaster this all was? How her pregnancy complicated everything?

"You can't go out with her," the king said.

"Why not?" Qadir asked. "I like her."

Words spoken to prove a point, she told herself. Silly words that meant nothing. Yet she wanted to wrap herself in them like they were a blanket and she were caught in a snowstorm. She felt her eyes burning, but refused to give in to tears.

"Maggie stays," Qadir said. "We will issue a discreet statement saying the child isn't mine."

"No one will believe you. Not until the child is born and there can be a DNA test."

"Perhaps not, but we will have stated our position. No one will publicly defy us. We will be left alone. Maggie will be left alone. That is what matters to me."

Mukhtar narrowed his gaze. "She means this much to you?"

"Yes."

"Very well. I hope you know what you're doing."

With that, the king left.

Maggie waited until he was out of the room to turn on Qadir. "Are you insane? What are doing? You can't go up against your father like that. It's crazy and wrong. I'm pregnant, Qadir. With another man's child. I know you don't want your father picking out your future wife, but this is taking things too far. I can't stay. Besides, you're a handsome, rich guy who happens to be a prince. Are you telling me there isn't one other woman you can think of to play this game?"

She practically spat the last couple of sentences at him. Her eyes flashed with temper so hot, he expected to see flames. Intriguing.

"So much energy," he told her.

"One of us has to put a little energy into this," she told him. "You obviously have a head injury. I am *pregnant*."

"Despite your repetitions of the facts, I am already aware of that."

The morning paper had shocked him, but not nearly as much as his reaction to the picture. He'd felt a deep, powerful sense of betrayal. As if he'd been cheated on.

Maggie was his in name only. There was nothing between them...if one ignored the powerful sexual chemistry that drew him at every turn. So why would he care that she was pregnant by another man?

Yet he found himself caring and that reaction was so unexpected, he wanted to know what it meant. So he wasn't going to let her go. Not yet.

"A month," he told her. "Stay a month. You can finish the car. If acting as if we are dating is still too difficult, you can leave and I will pay you the full amount for both jobs."

She started to speak, then stopped. He wondered if she was going to refuse the money. If she could. He knew there were money troubles in her past. It would only take him a few minutes to get someone to find out her exact financial situation. But he chose not to violate her privacy that way. Not until he had to.

"I'll finish the car," she said at last. "I want to do that. It means a lot to me."

"And the rest?"

"I can't figure out why you'd want to continue to pretend to date me, but it's your call. For now, I'll agree."

That night Maggie curled up on the sofa in Victoria's suite and sipped the herbal tea her friend had made. Her friend's rooms were similar to hers, with a stylish living room and French doors leading out to the balcony that wrapped around the palace.

But unlike Maggie, Victoria had added little touches to make the place her own. There were a few prints on the walls, a throw that added color. Colorful masks formed a centerpiece on the dining room table.

"They're beautiful," Maggie said. "Where did you find them?"

"The local bazaar. They mostly sell food, but a few times a year they feature work from local craftsmen. I always try to go. I've picked up some beautiful jewelry, as well. There's supposed to be a place in the desert where they make the most exquisite gold. Beautiful woven patterns, like nothing you've ever seen. I have a pair of earrings I—"

She started to stand, then sank back onto the sofa. "Sorry. You're not interested in my earrings."

"Not even on my best day," Maggie admitted with a smile. "But I can pretend."

"No need. I forgot the purpose of our meeting."

"That's right. I'm expecting you to fix my life."

"I'm not sure I'm up to that," Victoria told her.

"I know. It's kind of beyond fixing." Maggie set down her mug and pulled her knees to her chest. "I feel so awful. Not physically," she added quickly. "I'm fine. In fact if I didn't know better, I would swear I wasn't pregnant. Nothing's different. Shouldn't I be throwing up or something?"

"That can come later," her friend told her.

"Something to look forward to." Maggie sighed. "I just can't get my mind around the fact that I'm going to have a baby. I've been distracted the whole day, thinking about it, but it's just words. I don't know how to make it mean anything."

"You have time."

"Nine months less six weeks," Maggie said. "I know the day it happened. The exact day."

"The last time you were with Jon."

Maggie nodded.

"So you're confused," Victoria said. "That's not a surprise. You weren't expecting to end up pregnant. But beyond confusion…is there anything else?"

Maggie tried to probe her heart. What did she feel? "Terror," she admitted. "I'm not like you. I don't know how to be a mother."

Victoria held up both her hands. "Hey, I'm about the least maternal person you know. I can't keep a plant alive."

"But you're so feminine and girly."

"Knowing how to buy shoes on sale has nothing to do with being maternal. You're confusing your definitions of feminine. From what you've told me about your past, you'll be a great mother."

Maggie stared at her. "Why?"

"Because you had a great father. He was totally there for you. He loved you and supported you and only wanted what was best for you. So you know how to do the same. No baby is going to care if you actually knitted the blanket or bought it at a store. What he or she will care about is being loved. And you're gonna love your baby."

Maggie felt a twinge of something inside. Something hot and fierce and powerful. A baby. Was it possible?

"Thank you," she said. "You've made me feel better. So that's one problem down and four thousand left. I'm pregnant."

Victoria smiled. "I know."

"This is a huge complication."

"It usually is."

"I'm going to have to deal with Jon at some point."

"True."

"This isn't going to make him happy."

"You'll figure something out."

Maggie wasn't so sure, but she didn't want to think about Jon just then. "I felt bad about that picture being in the paper. It was incredibly humiliating for me, but I also felt awful about Qadir. That he got dragged into this."

Victoria sipped her tea. "An interesting way of looking at things. A case could be made that he dragged you into things by offering up the deal in the first place."

"He didn't know I was pregnant. He never would have said anything if he had."

"Agreed. My point is that he started things going by wanting to pretend to date you."

"Maybe. I just hate that now he has to deal with my problem."

"Because you like him."

"Of course I like him. He's a great guy. He defended me to the king."

Maggie still couldn't believe how Qadir had stood up for her. While she hated to cause trouble in the family, she couldn't help feeling safe and protected, even just for the moment.

"I find it fascinating that he still wants to see you," Victoria said. "Even after knowing you're pregnant by another man."

"I know. I don't get it, either. I told him we should break things off. That the public would totally understand him dumping me." She shivered slightly. "I'll admit I hated the idea of being branded a slut in the press, but I'm responsible for what I did, so it was only fair that I was the one who got stuck. I said I really wanted to finish the car, but nothing else."

"He didn't agree."

"I can't figure out why. What's in it for him? There's going to be speculation about the baby no matter what anyone says. I wonder if I made a mistake in agreeing."

"Isn't the bigger question whether or not Qadir made a mistake in asking you to stay."

Maggie didn't want to think about that, but she knew her friend was telling the truth. "Probably."

"But that's not the most interesting part," Victoria said. "What I find intriguing is that Prince Qadir of El Deharia, who could admittedly have nearly any woman he wanted, has chosen you."

Maggie straightened. "What?"

"He picked you to play the game for a lot of reasons. You're pretty, he thought he could spend time in your company without going crazy, that sort of thing. But it was a deal. A monetary transaction. Yet suddenly, it's more than that. When faced with trouble, instead of running, he's standing by you."

"He's just that kind of person."

Victoria laughed. "I promise you, if Nadim and I had the same kind of arrangement and I had turned up pregnant, he would have kicked me to the curb so fast there would be skid marks."

"Then why would you want to marry a man like that?"

Victoria sighed. "Good question. I had these big plans to marry for money and spend the rest of my life totally secure. But apparently I picked the wrong prince. The more I look at how Qadir is with you, the less I like Nadim. I've been working with him for two years and he hasn't noticed me. What kind of idiot is he?"

"One you should forget about. Do you really need to marry for money? What about love?"

"Love is for fools," Victoria said firmly. "I will never be a fool for love. But you're right about me forgetting Nadim. He may be a prince, but he's a boring twit of a man and I'm so over him."

Maggie grinned. "That would be a more impressive statement if you'd ever actually cared about him."

"I know." Victoria drank more of her tea. "Maybe I can find a nice diplomat in the foreign office. Someone who comes from money."

"Would you get off the money thing?"

"I can't. You don't know what it's like to be afraid you're going to lose everything. That's how I grew up. There were plenty of nights I watched my mother go hungry because there was only food for one. I vowed that I would never be like her—never give my heart to a jerk who walked on it and used her, thinking only of himself."

Maggie didn't know about her friend's past. "I'm sorry," she murmured. "I'm sorry you went through that."

"Me, too." Victoria sighed. "Wow—talk about getting carried away. I didn't mean to shift the conversation that way. We were talking about you. Have you considered that he defended you because he doesn't want you to leave?"

Maggie blinked several times. Victoria's words floated through her brain, forming images, then fading, but never disappearing completely.

"It can't be that," she said at last.

"Why not?"

Because... Because...

"He's just being kind."

Victoria wrinkled her nose. "He's a sheik, honey. Kind isn't one of the descriptors. Arrogant, powerful, determined. Those all work. But kind? No way."

Maggie knew her friend was right, which did leave that interesting question on the table. Why hadn't Qadir just dumped her when he'd found out about the baby?

"He wants his car finished."

"I don't mean any disrespect when it comes to your skills," Victoria said, "but couldn't he just hire someone else? You're good and all, but do you have a totally unique talent?"

Maggie wanted to defend herself, but she understood the other woman's point.

"Then I can't explain it," she admitted.

"Oh, I can," Victoria told her. "I would say you have a sheik who's interested."

"I don't think so," Maggie said automatically, even as she found herself almost wishing it were true. Qadir? Interested?

She knew there was a powerful attraction between them, but that was just one of those weird, unexplained things. He might want to sleep with her, but getting emotionally involved was very different. There had to be another reason.

"Trust me," Victoria told her. "I've seen male indifference. He's not showing it."

"I can't believe he wants anything from me but the deal we'd arranged."

"I don't know where he's going with this, either," Victoria told her. "But I do know one thing. If he wanted you gone, you would be. The fact that you're still here tells me he wants something more from you. The trick is going to be figuring out what."

Chapter Nine

Maggie worked carefully to pry the door panel from the door. The fit was perfect, which made her job more difficult but would allow the end results to be spectacular.

After a day of confusion and worry and not knowing what all she was going to do with her life, it felt good to be back with the car. Here the world was clear and everything made sense. She knew what to do and how to do it.

She turned back to the body of the vehicle and ran her hands along the sides.

"You're going to be stunning," she murmured. "Men will want you, other cars will want to be you."

"She's going to get a big head," Qadir said as he walked into the garage. "I'm not sure that's a good idea."

Maggie smiled at him, trying not to notice the funny feeling in her stomach or the way her heartbeat suddenly tripled. "I think you'll be able to handle her even if she gets conceited."

"Perhaps."

"I'm taking the doors apart. We'll be able to see if there's any interior damage. Then they can get repaired, replace any missing little parts, sand, prime and paint."

"Are you sure you should be doing all this?" he asked.

Huh? "It's part of my job. Not fixing the doors will make the rest of the car look funny."

"I was referring to your pregnancy. Is it safe for you to work here now?"

Oh. That. "I'm still the same person I was yesterday," she told him firmly. "I'll be careful about chemicals. I wasn't going to paint the car, anyway. I'll want to do some of the sanding by hand, but I'll wear a protective mask so I don't breathe in the particles. I'll avoid solvents. Otherwise, I should be fine. I'm just pregnant—I haven't morphed into an alien."

"If you are sure."

"I am." The last thing she needed was him having second thoughts about her doing the job. She desperately needed the money.

"Now you see why it is so much easier to hire a man," he said.

She narrowed her eyes. "If you weren't royal and my boss, I swear, I'd sock you for saying that."

He grinned. "Is it true."

"It's not true. Men have issues. They come in drunk, aren't responsible, pick fights."

"A lot of generalizations."

She smiled. "You mean like assuming a pregnancy is going to get in the way?"

"Point taken."

She leaned against the car. "So is yours. My dad would never have admitted it, but I know he would have agreed with you. We used to argue about treating men and women equally. He kept saying they were different halves of the same whole. Yet he didn't mind my being in a nontraditional job. I think he was even proud of it."

"I'm sorry I could not meet him."

"Me, too. You would have liked him." She smiled as she remembered her father meeting various clients. He never cared about how rich they were or how important. To him, everyone was the same. "I still miss him."

"You have a lifetime of memories to draw upon."

"I know. That helps."

"Would he have enjoyed knowing he would be a grandfather?"

"I hope so," she admitted. "I know he would have been disappointed by the circumstances. I'm hardly proud of them myself. But he would have been there for me and in the end he would have been happy about the baby. He liked kids a lot. He would have been a great grandpa."

"Did he like Jon?"

"Yes. They were close. He always thought we'd be a good match. I think that's part of the reason we stayed together through his illness. Even when things weren't great between us, we didn't want to disappoint him." And Jon hadn't wanted to leave her alone.

She'd sensed that perhaps even before he'd been able to articulate the problem.

"Jon stood by me through the end and at the funeral. His parents also helped with so much."

The two families had been connected. That had been part of the problem, too. She and Jon had been walking away from more than just each other.

"When will you tell him?" Qadir asked.

Maggie folded her arms across her chest. "I don't know."

He didn't say anything. He didn't have to. She could give herself the lecture well enough for both of them.

Jon was the father of her child. He deserved to know there was a baby. He was a good man and he hadn't done anything wrong. She owed him the truth. But…

"I don't want to mess up his life," she admitted slowly. "Knowing about the baby is going to change everything. He's happy with Elaine. This is the last thing either of them need."

He continued to study her. She sighed.

"I know, I know. I'll tell him."

"What do you think he'll say?" he asked.

"I have no idea. He's big on family. I don't think he can just walk away."

"Is that what you want?"

"It would be easier for all of us if he would."

"Life is rarely easy."

"Agreed. It's just…a baby will connect us forever. How are we supposed to get on with our lives while we're so closely tied together?"

"Because you are still in love with him?"

"No. I'm not. I'm long over him." She'd been over him before that last night together. She just hadn't realized it yet. "But it creates tension and pressure. No matter who he marries, there will always be this child between them. She may be the first wife, but she won't have the first child. That will be forever taken from her."

"Does that matter?"

"I don't know. I think, for a man, his first child is very important. There's the whole pride thing. Telling the world he procreated. It's different for women."

"Having a child with someone else would still be significant for you?"

"Yes."

"Perhaps it will be so for Jon, as well."

"I hope so," Maggie said. She just wished she didn't have to deal with this at all. She got a knot in her stomach every time she thought about having to make that phone call.

"I wish he would just walk away," she murmured.

"Will he?"

"I don't think so."

How ironic. A few weeks ago she would have done anything to get him back in her life. Now she had the perfect opportunity and she wasn't interested.

"But you would like him to."

She nodded.

He moved forward and put his arm around her. "If there is anything I can do, you must tell me."

He was warm and strong. Talk about tempting, she thought, fighting the need to throw herself against him and beg him to handle everything. She knew he was more than capable. But this was her problem and she had to fix it herself.

"Thank you. You've already done so much."

He smiled at her. "I have done very little."

He released her. She forced herself to step away.

"There is a museum opening next week," he said. "I would like you to come with me to the event."

She took a second step back. "I don't think that's a good idea."

"We have a deal."

"One you should be rethinking. Honestly, Qadir, you don't want to go there."

"The longer we are together, the more serious the relationship will appear."

She pointed to her stomach. "Do we have to have the 'baby on board' discussion again?"

"Once you leave, people will believe the child is not mine. That will solve the problem." He looked determined. "I want to see this through. You promised to give me at least a month. I will hold you to that, Maggie."

She nodded slowly. Her reluctance came not only from the potential embarrassment to herself, but also from a tiny ache deep inside. She knew that Qadir was only using their relationship to fake out his father. Nothing more. Having him talk about that shouldn't bother her.

But it did. It hurt and for the life of her, she couldn't say why.

"And if I order you not to see her anymore?" the king demanded.

"I do not think that is a conversation you wish to have," Qadir told his father.

"What is the point of this? Why her? Find someone else. Someone who isn't carrying another man's child. What will happen if things progress? Will you marry her? Am I to accept that child as a grandchild?"

"As'ad is adopting three daughters," Qadir said. "You have no problem with them."

"That is totally different."

"Why?"

"It is. Everyone knew of the girls before. They are charming."

"Perhaps Maggie's baby will be charming, too."

His father glared at him. "You are being deliberately difficult."

"I am not, despite how it seems to you. Maggie is important to me. She is someone with whom I enjoy spending time. She is charming and amusing. She does not annoy me."

"An important consideration," the king said.

"Very. She is also not interested in the trappings of my position. My being a prince does not impress her."

"Like Whitney."

There were very few people who were allowed to speak that name. Unfortunately the king was one of them.

"Like Whitney," Qadir agreed. "But with one important difference. I do not love her. I like her. I respect her. But she does not possess my heart."

No one would again, he reminded himself. Once had been enough. He had loved Whitney beyond what he thought was possible and in the end, she had left him.

He'd been stunned by her decision and the emotional pain that had followed. He'd vowed then that no woman would ever bring him to his knees again.

"A sensible match between compatible parties makes the most sense," his father said. "But this woman? What about the child? He or she can never be heir."

"I am not the eldest son."

"Perhaps not, but if Kateb walks away, you will be next in line."

There was bitterness in his father's voice, and perhaps sadness. "Kateb means no disrespect. He has taken a different path."

"Into the desert. He belongs here."

"I do not agree." Qadir knew his brother could never be fully happy in the city. The desert sand ran in his veins. He was only truly alive when he was there.

"You seek to defy me at every turn it seems," Mukhtar grumbled. "I am disappointed in you, my son."

Qadir looked at his father and smiled. "You are not. You are annoyed by my refusal to do as you say, but you are secretly pleased that I will stand up to you fearlessly. It reminds you that you are an excellent father and monarch."

One corner of the other man's mouth twitched. "Perhaps. But that does not mean I approve of your relationship with Maggie.

You will get distracted by her, then decide she will not do. By then it will be too late. You will be interested. So when you send her away, you will not be interested in another woman for months."

"I do not see that happening," Qadir said, lying cheerfully. With luck, his plan was going to work perfectly.

Maggie sat in the gardens, her eyes closed, her body absorbing the heat of the sun. It was still early spring, so the temperature wasn't too hot. Compared to what the weather would be like back in Aspen, with snow and slush everywhere, this was paradise.

Unfortunately her reluctance to go inside had nothing to do with the pleasant surroundings and everything to do with what would happen when she got back to her room.

Before she could persuade herself not to put off calling Jon for another minute, a tall man in traditional clothing swept into the garden. He moved purposefully, taking long strides, his robes swirling behind him. While he was handsome, there was a deep scar on one cheek and an air of power about him. He was not the sort of man Maggie would want to argue with.

When he saw her, he came to a stop.

"An unexpected flower in my father's garden," he said.

That made Maggie laugh. "I'm not feeling especially flowery today, but thank you."

"Who are you?"

"Maggie Collins."

"Ah, yes. The woman who restores cars."

While they were guessing identities, she said, "And you would be Kateb, the mysterious brother who lives in the desert."

Kateb bowed low, then straightened. "Does my brother still speak of me with awe?"

She laughed. "Not so I'd noticed."

"Then you must listen harder."

He sat on the stone bench across from hers. Although they were outside and, in theory, not lacking in space, he seemed to fill up an excess of area.

"You are enjoying your time in El Deharia?" he asked.

"Yes. The country is beautiful. I haven't seen that much of it, but I hope to soon."

"Perhaps Qadir will show you his favorite places."

Maggie eyed the other man. Did he know about her deal with Qadir?

"Perhaps," she murmured.

"Do you often come out to the garden?" he asked.

"No. I'm avoiding something I know I have to do. Not my most mature decision of the day."

"But you will do what has to be done?"

She sighed, then nodded. "Yes, I'll do the right thing."

Kateb stared at her. "Do you always?"

"It's usually a goal. Is it the same for you?" she asked, knowing she probably shouldn't but wanting to ruffle Kateb's steely composure.

"When it suits me."

"How convenient."

"It is. I am Prince Kateb of El Deharia. I do as I please."

She laughed. "My father would say you're the kind of man whose mouth is writing checks the rest of him can't cash, but in your case, I'm going to guess you're telling the truth."

"Your father sounds like a sensible man."

"He was." She stood. "It was nice to meet you, Prince Kateb of El Deharia. If you'll excuse me, I have a phone call to make."

"The one you've been avoiding?"

She nodded.

He rose and bowed again. "I have enjoyed our conversation, Maggie Collins. My brother is more fortunate than he realizes."

•

* * *

Maggie watched the clock, then at the appointed time, she picked up the phone and dialed a familiar number. She and Jon had e-mailed back and forth to set up the call. She'd told him speaking with him was important but hadn't said why.

"Maggie," he said when he answered. "What's wrong?"

"Nothing. I'm fine."

"I've been worried."

"I said everything was okay."

"I know, but I couldn't think of why you'd need to talk to me unless something was wrong. Is everything all right there? Do you need anything?"

She needed to be able to turn back time and undo that single night, she thought sadly. Or did she? Although she was terrified about being pregnant and had no idea what the next seven and a half months would bring, she couldn't bring herself to regret the baby.

"I'm doing great," she told him. "Work on the car is going well. I'm enjoying the country. It's different but wonderful. Plus I'm living in a palace. How often does that happen?"

"Are you sure? I could probably get some time off and come get you."

She frowned. "Jon, I can take care of myself."

"I'm not convinced."

Wait a minute. How long had he seen her as incapable? She sure didn't like that.

"You should be. I'm a big girl. All grown-up. Let's change the subject. How's Elaine?"

There was a moment of silence. She wasn't sure if he didn't want to let go of how she might need him or if he was uncomfortable talking about Elaine.

"She's fine."

"You're still going out?"

"Yes."

"Come on, Jon. Details. Are things getting serious?"

"Sort of." He drew in a breath. "They are. She's funny. She wants a cat. She's wanted one for a long time, but her roommate was allergic. The roommate got married a couple of weeks ago, so Elaine has the apartment to herself, but she still hasn't gotten a cat. I finally asked her why and she said she wanted to make sure it was okay with me. I told her it was her cat."

Men weren't always as bright as they could be, Maggie thought humorously. "She wants to make sure you like cats, too."

"Yeah, I got that later. It was kind of cool, you know, that my opinion mattered that much."

"Is she getting the cat?"

"We're going to pick one out over the weekend."

"I'm glad."

Maggie said the words, then braced herself for a twinge. She and Jon had never gotten to the pet-sharing stage. But all she felt was pleasure for him.

"Sounds like things are getting serious," she said. "That's good. I hope you two are really happy together."

"Maggie, I..."

"Jon, don't worry about me. I'm fine. We're over. We were over a long time before we ended things. I wish we could have seen that. I know we stayed together because of my dad and while I'm sure he appreciated the gesture, we weren't doing ourselves any favors."

"I don't want to hurt you."

"I'm not hurt. We had a great few years and I'll always be grateful but we're growing in different directions." She knew he liked taking care of people and hoped Elaine enjoyed being taken care of by him.

Unfortunately things were not going to get easier for any of them.

"I want to talk to you about that last time we were together," she said, hating that she had to bring it up.

"Maggie, don't. We're both to blame."

"Me a little more than you."

"I didn't have to come over."

"I made a pass at you," she said, wishing it wasn't true. "I seduced you."

"I let myself be seduced. I guess we both wanted that one last time. My only regret is if it hurt you. Otherwise I'm glad we were together."

Maybe he had been, but all that was about to change.

"You're beating yourself up over nothing," he continued. "Maggie, you have to let it go."

"I wish I could," she said softly. "But it's not that simple." She drew in a breath. "I'm pregnant, Jon. After we stopped seeing each other, I went off the pill. I wasn't expecting anything to happen, so why bother? I just never thought about it."

She paused to give him a chance to speak but there was only silence on the other end of the phone. She knew him well enough to imagine the shocked look on his face.

She decided to say the little speech she'd prepared while he was trying to figure out what the hell had just gone wrong with his life.

"I know this is totally unexpected," she said. "Neither of us ever imagined this happening. But it did. I also know that you're a total good guy and you'll feel responsible. Jon, you're not. I'm the one to blame and I'm the one who is going to deal with this."

Now came the hard part. "I don't want anything from you. I mean that. You have a life, a great woman and a future. Having a baby with me will only mess that up. I told you about the baby because you have the right to know, but that's the only reason. I have no expectations. What I'm really hoping is that you'll walk away and live your life. You don't have to be involved. We can find a lawyer to write up some papers. You sign away all your rights and I promise to never come after you for money. Considering what has happened between us, it's really the best decision."

She paused again and there was still silence. She couldn't figure out what that meant.

"I know you need time to think about all this. You've been blindsided by something really huge. Fortunately we have time." She sighed. "I'm so sorry. I never meant for this to happen. I didn't do it on purpose."

"I know that," he said at last, his voice low and thick with emotion. "Dammit, Maggie, are you sure?"

She winced. "I took three different pregnancy tests. They all came out positive. I'm sure."

"I'm not blaming you," he said. "Either of us could have walked away. I meant what I said before. I wanted that last time with you."

"Just not the consequences."

"I didn't say that."

He didn't have to. In his position, she would be angry and confused. What to do? Where to go? What about Elaine?

"You need to think about what I said," she told him. "About just walking away. I know it won't be your first instinct, but it's the right thing to do. I'm perfectly capable of raising a child on my own."

"You need to come home."

Uh-oh. Was he going to get all parental on her? "I'm fine. I'm perfectly healthy. If you're worried about the baby, I can find a doctor here."

"You need to come home," he repeated. "Not for the doctor, but so we can get married."

Chapter Ten

Qadir walked into the usually quiet garage and watched as Maggie threw tools into the large open box on the floor.

"Just so damn *stupid,*" she muttered. "Does anyone care about my opinion? *Noooo.* I just want to beat him with a stick."

She threw more tools as she grumbled, her expression tight with annoyance, her movements jerky. She was on fire and he found himself attracted to her temper.

"Someone has annoyed you," he said.

She turned and glared at him. "Yes, someone has. A man. You probably don't want to be here today, what with you being a man and all. I'm angry enough not to be picky about who I yell at."

He laughed. "You do not frighten me."

"Because I'm a woman, right? What is it with you men that you think you know better?" She pointed to his crotch. "It's just excess flesh, you know. It's not the great repository for all knowledge. Since when did being a man make you an oracle?"

She was all fire and rage. Both her passion and beauty excited him.

"I did not claim to be an oracle," he told her. "I said I am not afraid of you."

"You should be." She picked up a large wrench. "I could do a lot of damage with that."

"Yes, you could." He walked over and removed it from her grasp, then set it on the desk. Still holding her hand in his, he rubbed her fingers. "What happened?"

"I talked to Jon."

Qadir did not respond. Better for Maggie to tell him in her own way.

She drew in a breath. "He's just so annoying. His stupid superior attitude. Like he has all the answers. I hate that."

"And him?"

"I don't hate him, but I want to smack him upside the head. He's convinced he knows best. Since when does he get to be in charge of my life? Hello, it's my life. Mine. Not his. But will he accept that? I'll give you one guess on that question."

Qadir had not been pleased to know that Maggie would have to tell the other man about the baby, but there was little choice in the matter.

She looked at him. "He wants to marry me."

"He is an honorable man," he told her, enjoying a brief image of crushing Jon like a bug. "That should please you."

"Well, it doesn't. It really pisses me off. Okay, fine. I'll accept he wants to be a part of his child's life. Knowing him, I shouldn't be surprised. I still think it would be better if he walked away, but he won't. That's just so him. But marriage? Did he notice the new-century thing, because here we are. It's a shiny new world and by God, no man is going to marry me just because I'm pregnant with his child."

The marriage proposal did not come as a surprise, but Qadir did not like it.

"He doesn't even care that it's not what I want," Maggie continued, still fuming. "No. It's all about him and the baby and what's right." She turned on Qadir. "How is this right? How is two people making themselves miserable right? Wait. It's not two people. It's three. What about Elaine? I think they're falling in love and he's going to toss that away because of the baby? This is just so typical. Do you know he doesn't think I'm capable? I never got that before, but he just about said I couldn't do this on my own. That really, really annoys me."

She jerked free of his touch and stalked around the car. "It's a guy thing, right? The need to assume women are just a little bit less? Why is that? Do we threaten you so damn much? Oh, I'm just so mad I could spit."

Despite potential risk to his person, Qadir chuckled. She turned on him.

"You think this is funny?"

"I think you are beautiful and full of life. Jon is a fool for ever letting you go, but that is his loss. He must deal with it now."

Her eyes widened. "That was good," she breathed. "Seriously. I feel almost disarmed."

"How unfortunate, as I like you armed. Go to your office and get changed. I will take you to lunch and then shopping. You will feel better when we are finished."

She rolled her eyes. "And here I was starting to like you. Do you get that I'm not the shopping type?"

"I haven't said what we're shopping for."

"Oh. Well, if it's cars, I'm so there."

He smiled. "Go get changed."

"Okay. It would probably be better for me to get out than to stay here."

"Agreed. I do not want you taking out your temper on my Rolls."

She laughed, then closed the door behind her. Qadir stayed where he was, careful not to move because if he did, he would join her in her office and this time when he touched her, he would not stop.

An impossible situation, he told himself. At first Maggie had intrigued him with her humor and lack of pretension. He had enjoyed her company, but nothing more. Recently, though, he thought they might become lovers. The chemistry between them would make their time together pass very quickly. He had considered discussing that with her, but now everything was different.

She was pregnant and the father of her child wanted to marry her. Qadir knew he could not stand between them, even when his gut told him Jon was not the one for her. Jon had let her get away. What had the other man been thinking, to prefer another woman over Maggie? Impossible.

Not that he would be having that conversation with Jon anytime soon. But it gave Qadir pleasure to imagine the other man's fear when faced with a powerful sheik.

He wondered if Maggie could be convinced to accept Jon's proposal. He did not think so, but what did he really know of a woman's mind? Perhaps she secretly longed for her old lover.

He didn't want to think about that, about her being with someone else, so he pushed the image away. For now, and for as long as he wanted her, Maggie was his. Yet he had only bought her time. Did Jon still possess her heart?

"Better," Maggie said as they walked out of the restaurant. "That was exactly what I needed."

"You have an impressive appetite," Qadir said.

"I know. It gets embarrassing. I've always thought that if my work weren't so physical, I would blow up like a balloon. Which, at this moment, I don't care about."

For the first time since her uncomfortable conversation with Jon, she felt as if she could catch her breath. Maybe it was that big, juicy hamburger sitting in her stomach. A burger, fries and a shake had been exactly what she'd needed to change her mood.

"Thank you," she told the man at her side.

"You are welcome. Although I enjoy watching you throw things, I like seeing you smile, as well."

She looked up at him, at his dark eyes, his handsome features. "You're really smooth."

"I know."

"It's a prince thing, isn't it?"

"Some of it is me. My cousin Nadim is also a prince, but he is completely lacking in personality."

"I talked to him at the ball. He was a lot more formal than you."

"A kind way of ignoring his shortcomings."

Maggie hadn't been impressed, either, which made her wonder why Victoria would even consider marrying him. Yes, he was a prince and all, but marriage was forever. Especially a royal one.

Qadir put his arm around her and pulled her close. "I, however, have a wonderful personality and you are completely charmed by me."

"That's true," she said with a laugh, even as she leaned into him. She liked it when he held her or touched her. Her body melted as little nerve endings began a "touch me" dance in the strangest places.

She wanted to turn to him and have him kiss her. Deep kisses like before with lips and tongue and hot breath. She wanted to be swept away and taken and…

Oh God. She was pregnant. Pregnant with another man's child. She couldn't have erotic thoughts about Qadir. It wasn't right. It was borderline icky.

He was totally the wrong man and even if he wasn't, her being pregnant made her the wrong woman.

The good news was her attraction to him was purely physical. It wasn't as if her heart had gotten involved at all.

They headed back for the car. Qadir had driven and parked at the end of the block. But before they reached the gleaming Mercedes, she caught sight of a window display.

Last week she never would have noticed it, but today she slowed as she took in the pale green blanket draped over the white rocking chair. The small-scale dresser had painted rabbits playing together on the drawers. A toy box stood open with stuffed animals spilling from it.

Maggie slowed, then stopped. "I've never been in a baby store before," she whispered.

"Would you like to go in now?"

It probably wasn't the shopping he'd had in mind, but she nodded anyway, then hesitated before stepping through the open door.

"Is this okay?" she asked.

"Yes."

She could see displays set up like rooms, with cribs and tables. Changing tables, she told herself, having no idea where that information had come from.

He dropped his hand to the small of her back and gave her a little push. She stepped through the door.

The space was huge and filled with clothes and toys, supplies and furniture. Maggie walked in a few feet, then stopped, not sure what to look at first.

"I don't think I can do this," she murmured.

Qadir came up beside her. "You do not have to do anything today. That should make things easier. We will walk around and get some ideas. Later, you can decide about what you need. Think of this as the first visit to the showroom. You're not buying a car today."

The analogy was perfect and helped her relax. She smiled at him. "Did I mention you're good?"

"Several times, but it is praise I enjoy so feel free to say it again."

Without thinking, she leaned against him. He wrapped his arms around her and kissed her cheek. She raised her head for a real kiss, hoping he would—

"Prince Qadir, what an honor. I am Fatima. Welcome to my store."

The speaker was a pretty woman in her thirties. She beamed at both of them, clasping her hands together. Maggie's stomach knotted and she instantly regretted the hamburger.

"It is a pleasure to meet you," Qadir said smoothly.

Maggie stepped back and cleared her throat. What was she supposed to say? Her pregnancy had been reported in the newspaper and showing up here, like this, would only cause people to think Qadir really *was* the father.

"We, ah, were just looking around," she said, wishing she didn't sound so lame.

"Of course. Please. Explore. If you have any questions I will be at the front desk."

Fatima gave a little bob, then hurried away. Maggie watched her go.

"I'm sorry," she said, feeling awful. "We shouldn't have come in here."

"Why not?"

"Because of what people will think."

"You are having a child."

"But not *yours,*" she said, trying not to shriek. "That's what they will think."

"We know the truth."

He sounded so calm. "You're not upset?"

"No." He took her hand. "Come on. Let us explore, as Fatima suggested. Based on all I see here, an infant needs far more than his size suggests."

She thought about pointing out all the potentials for disaster, but knew Qadir would understand them far better than she. If he could be calm about this, then she could, too.

"Just to be clear," she told him. "I'm having a girl."

"You are confident about that?"

"Yes. I sense my body would reject boy sperm."

"Then Jon is weak for not overpowering you."

"Or sensible for not trying."

They walked around the various displays. One showed a room done in trains, with everything from an adorable locomotive border print to stuffed train pillows. There was also a car room and one done totally in pink with a ballerina motif.

"If you're having a girl," Qadir said, pointing at the dancer.

Maggie glared at him. "Don't make me hit you in public."

"You are not as tough as you think."

"Cheap talk while you're safely around other people."

He smiled slowly. "You do not intimidate me in any way, Maggie. We both know how easily I could take you."

She wasn't sure if he was referring to his superior strength or the way her body responded every time he touched her and she wasn't sure it mattered. He was right—he could take her without breaking a sweat. The only news in that was how much she wanted him to.

"Maybe this is better," he said, pointing to a display done in shades of yellow. The teddy bear theme wasn't too sweet and she liked the border print with the teddy bears playing different sports.

"I could live with this," she said, walking around the area, touching the crib and running her hands across the top of the dresser. "The yellow is nice. I'm not a huge fan of green and we all know I'm not doing a pink-on-pink room."

"You're going to have some explaining to do if the child is male."

She smiled. "I know, but I'll be very smug when it's a girl."

"I would have sons."

"Oh, please. Is this also a prince thing?"

"No. Biology. My aunt is the only female child born in several generations."

"Oh. I hadn't thought of that." But this wasn't Qadir's baby, so she didn't have to worry.

They wandered through the rest of the store. Maggie started to hyperventilate when they stopped in front of a wall of baby items and she had no idea what they were for.

"Do they come with instructions?" she asked in a whisper.

"I am sure they do."

She pointed to a small container with a cord and a plug. "A baby wipe heater? Their wipes have to be heated?" She hadn't known that. What if there was a power outage and the wipes were cold? Would that hurt the baby?

Panic filled her. "I can't do this," she said, placing her hand on her stomach. "I'm sorry, but I really, really can't do this. I don't know how. I'll do a lousy job. What if I don't like children?"

Qadir put his hand on her shoulder. "You will be fine."

"You're just saying that because you don't want me hysterical. You don't actually know."

"I know you are intelligent and caring and you will love your child. What else matters?"

"Heated baby wipes, for one thing. What else don't I know?"

"You will learn as you go."

"Maybe. But what if I don't? What if my child is the only one with a cold butt?"

His mouth twitched. She balled up her fist and socked him in the arm. "You'd better not be laughing at me."

He chuckled, then pulled her against him and kissed her. His mouth brushed hers once, twice, then he released her.

"You are a unique woman," he told her.

"Uniquely unqualified to be a mother."

He took her hand and led her to the rows of books. "If you do not know what to do, you can learn about it."

"Oh, right. Books." She picked up one and scanned the title. "I need one for women who have no experience with children. Something like—'You've never had a baby before, but that's okay.' Do you see that title?"

He held up several that weren't even close, but she grabbed them all. Something to fill her nights, she thought.

Qadir insisted on paying for the books—which was only going to fuel speculation, she thought as they left. When they were back in his car, she turned to him.

"Thank you for being so nice," she said. "You're really easy to be around."

"You are, as well," he told her. "I enjoyed our outing."

"Even though there's going to be an article or two in the paper tomorrow."

"Even though."

She told herself to say something else, to look away, to make a joke. But she couldn't. She seemed caught up in his gaze, in the power of the man. Breathing was difficult and thinking was impossible. What on earth was wrong with her?

"You were brilliant," Maggie told Victoria as they walked back to their rooms. "I had no idea what to get a princess for her wedding shower. The lingerie was beautiful."

Victoria had suggested they go in together for Kayleen's present and had offered to do the shopping.

"She didn't register, which was probably about her marrying a prince. I'm guessing the royal set would see that as tacky. Plus, hey, what could a princess want? Cookware? So I went with the easy gift. Something sexy."

"More than sexy." The lace and silk nighties had been stunning. "Kayleen looked happy."

"An important consideration," Victoria teased. "One wants to stay on the good side of a future royal."

Maggie knew her friend was right, but the whole situation was beyond imagining. "A month ago I was in Aspen working for a friend in his garage. I'd never been out of the country. I'd barely left the state. Now I'm here, having just attended a wedding shower for a future princess. We're in a palace. There is a seriously surreal quality to my life these days."

"I know," Victoria admitted as they took the stairs to the second floor. "Most of the time I'm totally used to all this, but every now and then I look around and wonder how a girl like me landed here. It's a question I haven't answered yet. Of course, I don't have your complication."

Maggie knew what the other woman was talking about. "Qadir isn't a complication."

"Oh, really. What would you call him?"

"My boss."

"Whom you're pretending to date, while pregnant."

A good point, Maggie thought.

"Just be careful," Victoria told her. "Watch yourself."

Maggie knew that was good advice. A couple of weeks ago she would have brushed it off. Be careful for what? She was fine. But now…

Victoria paused on the landing and looked at her. "What?" she asked sharply. "You're not telling me I'm worrying for nothing. You're not saying he's just your boss."

"He's just my boss."

"Oh, that was convincing."

Maggie climbed the rest of the stairs. Victoria followed. Once they were in the corridor, Maggie shrugged. "He might be a complication."

"Okay. Why?"

"I don't know. I feel funny when I'm around him."

"Funny as in slightly sick to your stomach mingling with a strong need to throw yourself at him and beg to be taken?"

"Maybe."

"Oh, man, that's not good." Victoria looked at her. "You like him."

"He's a great guy. I enjoy his company, that's all. It's just that I don't have a lot of friends here."

"Great. He turns you on *and* you're trying to rationalize the situation. That is never good. I was going to say you're falling for him, but I think it's too late for that. You've fallen and hard."

Maggie wanted to protest that wasn't possible, but there was a sense of rightness in her friend's words. A rightness that scared her down to her bones.

"I can't fall for him," she whispered. "It would be a huge mistake. He's a prince. I'm pregnant. Worse, I'm a mechanic. Guys like him don't marry women like me. They marry socialites and beauty queens."

"Get out while the getting is good," Victoria told her.

"I can't leave. I need the money. My dad's cancer totally wiped us out financially. I have nothing in the bank. I need the money from restoring the car to help me get through the pregnancy and beyond. I won't be able to work right after."

"I have some money saved," Victoria began.

Maggie smiled at her friend. "Thanks, but no. You've worked hard for what you have. I just have to be sensible. I can pull back. I wasn't paying attention with Qadir. He's funny and caring and I let myself get sucked in. I won't do that anymore. I'll be on guard."

"A good plan," Victoria said slowly. "There's only one problem. I've never heard any of the princes being described as funny and caring."

"Maybe I'm seeing a side of him he keeps hidden."

"Or maybe you're in more trouble than you thought."

That night Maggie couldn't sleep. There was too much on her mind. Every time she thought about her conversation with Jon she got annoyed all over again, which didn't help with relaxing. But when she tried to think about something else, her thoughts wandered to Qadir.

She appreciated Victoria's warning. Maggie hadn't realized she was in danger. Now that she understood the problem, she could do a better job of protecting herself emotionally. No more long lunches or shopping trips. She would be his mechanic, nothing more.

Around midnight, she gave up pretending she would doze off, pulled on jeans and a T-shirt, but no bra, and stepped out onto the balcony.

The night was clear and balmy with a hint of the summer heat that would soon follow. She could see stars and smell the sea. There were sounds in the distance, but the palace grounds themselves were quiet.

She moved quietly through the night to one of her favorite spots—a seating area that jutted out over the water. During the day there were often people there, drinking coffee, talking, but at this time of night, the space was empty.

Maggie ignored the cluster of chairs and walked to the railing. She leaned against it and stared down at the dark, swirling water. The sound of the sea soothed her. It reminded her that whatever her problems were at the moment, life went on. She could ride the tide or she could fight it, but in the end, the tide would win.

"We're going to figure this out," she whispered to the tiny life inside her. "Don't you worry. I'm working on a plan."

"Do you need help with it?"

She turned and saw a tall man behind her. It was too dark to see his features, but her heart recognized him all too well.

"Qadir."

"I could not sleep," he told her. "When that happens, I come here."

She didn't know what to say. They were having a fairly normal conversation, so words should come easily. But her recent talk with Victoria had changed things. She was aware of her possible growing feelings, of how she no longer thought of Qadir as just her boss. She was afraid her interest would show and he would be kind. Sometimes kindness could be the worst.

He stepped closer. "Are you all right?" he asked.

She nodded.

"What troubles you?"

"Nothing," she murmured. "I'm fine."

A light wind blew a strand of hair across her face. He reached out, probably to tuck it behind her ear. But the second his fingers brushed against her skin, she felt her whole body go up in flames. Need pulsed through her, a heady rhythm that blocked out the sound of the sea.

She stared at him, wanting to get lost in his dark eyes. While he didn't promise to be a safe haven, she knew he would protect her for as long as she was in his arms. Right now that seemed like more than enough.

She wanted him to touch her, to hold her, drawing her close, taking her with a passion that would leave them both breathless.

He cupped her cheek. "In a foolish attempt to be honorable, I will tell you that I am no longer willing to walk away from the temptation you offer."

Meaning she should be the one to leave. That if they started something, they wouldn't stop.

Her heart fluttered and her skin burned. Anticipation swept through her making her melt from the inside out.

"Maggie."

He said her name with a low growl that made her shiver.

Two clear choices. Be sensible or give in. She knew what she *should* do and what she *wanted* to do. In the end, it wasn't a choice at all.

Slowly, carefully, so there could be no question of her intent, she rose on tiptoe and kissed him.

Chapter Eleven

Maggie waited what seemed like a lifetime before Qadir responded to her kiss. She was just starting to think she'd made a huge mistake when he drew back and stared at her.

"I don't want to hurt you," he admitted.

Relief was as sweet as it was intense. "I can handle it," she said with a smile.

"So you claim."

"Test me."

He took her hand in his and led the way to an open French door halfway down the long balcony. They stepped inside what she assumed was his room, but didn't get much of a chance to explore.

The second the door closed behind them, he pulled her close and claimed her with a kiss that burned her down to the soles of her feet.

His lips took all she offered and more. His tongue swept

inside, exploring, claiming, urging. She met him stroke for stroke as need grew, filling her, making her ache and want.

He touched her everywhere, first up and down her back, then down her rear where he cupped the curves. She moved against him, feeling his erection, loving how hard he felt, wishing he were inside her already.

He broke their kiss long enough to pull off her T-shirt, then he cupped her bare breasts in his hands.

Even as his fingers worked their magic on her sensitive nipples, he kissed her all over her face. His mouth moved along her jaw, then down to her neck where he licked and nipped and made her gasp.

Liquid desire poured through her. She was already wet and swollen and when he bent down to suck on her breasts, she gasped her pleasure.

She touched him where she could. His hard muscles rippled in response to her caress. She was about to tell him to take off his shirt when he dropped to his knees. At the same time he unfastened her jeans, then jerked them and her panties down to her ankles.

She was trapped by her clothing, unable to step away or spread her legs very far apart. Still he kissed her stomach, then parted her with his fingers before kissing her intimately.

The feel of his lips and tongue was exquisite. She had to hang on to him to keep from falling to the floor. He found her center and licked it over and over again as he moved his hands behind her and squeezed her curves.

"Qadir," she breathed, wanting what he was doing to go on forever, but needing more. A bed, she thought frantically. A sofa. The floor.

Still loving her between her thighs, he helped her out of her shoes, then eased her clothes from her body. She opened her legs more, giving him access, desperate to give in to the building pressure.

She put her hands on his shoulders and hung on for the ride. But just as she was about to surrender and lose herself in pleasure, he stood.

"You can't stop," she gasped.

"I'm just getting started."

He led her down a hallway, into a large bedroom. She had a brief impression of dark, masculine furniture and a bed that could sleep twenty. Then Qadir pulled back the covers, turned to her and began to touch her.

"You are so beautiful," he murmured, stroking her back. "All of you. It's maddening to watch you prance around in your coveralls with those little fitted T-shirts. I have dreamed about you in that T-shirt and nothing else."

Heat filled her as his words aroused her to the brink. He'd fantasized about *her?* Was that possible?

"I don't prance," she said, trying to tease rather than give in to unexpected tears. She couldn't figure out why on earth those words would make her want to cry, but they did.

"You excite me beyond what I can say."

He was doing a pretty good job of exciting her, as well.

She reached for the buttons on his shirt, but he pushed her hands away. As she watched, he undressed, revealing his hard, honey-colored skin.

As he pushed down his briefs, she saw his arousal—all jutting maleness that called to her. Her pulled her close and they tumbled onto the big bed, a tangle of arms and legs and need.

Even as he took her breast into his mouth, he reached between her legs and stroked her.

He found that one sensitive spot instantly and circled it. She didn't know what to think about first—his mouth or his fingers. Both were exquisite, pushing her higher, driving her closer to her release.

The steady rhythm—his sucking, his touching, her body pulsing—threatened to push her over the edge. She held back, not wanting to give in so quickly. Then he shifted so he was between her thighs, kissing her with his tongue again. He pushed a finger inside of her, circling, thrusting, rubbing and she was lost.

Her release carried her to the edge of the world and let her go. Every muscle shuddered with pleasure, making her cry out. On and on until she floated back to earth, back to his bed where she opened her eyes and found him watching her.

Despite the fact that she might never be able to move again, fire still burned. Without saying anything, she held open her arms. He eased between her legs, his hardness filling her, stretching her, making her cling to him.

He made love to her like a man starved. Deep thrusts claimed her as his and she held on for the ride of her life. His excitement pulled her along, making her hungry, as well. Her body tensed and ached and when he stiffened, she, too, cried out, feeling more satisfied than she'd ever been before.

Later, when they were together under the covers, her body pressed against his, his hands stroking her head, he kissed her.

"I am sorry," he said. "I tried to hold back. I did not want to hurt you."

"You didn't."

"I took you roughly."

He wouldn't meet her gaze, as if he was ashamed.

She rolled on top of him, pressing her body to his, then kissed him. "Qadir, didn't you feel me responding? I'm not saying I want to be hurt. Your passion excited me. Isn't that how it's supposed to be?"

"I should have more control."

She smiled. "No, you shouldn't."

He put his hands on her hips and eased her down. He was hard again. She slid over him, taking him inside of her. She gasped at the pleasure of it.

"Perhaps if you were in charge," he told her, need once again burning between them.

She braced herself on the bed. He reached for her breasts, then lightly teased her nipples. Sensation shot through her. She rode him up and down, then moving faster and faster. They both groaned.

It was, she thought as her body clenched in anticipation, going to be an amazing night.

Maggie supposed that technically she walked back to her room the next morning, but in truth it felt like floating. Her whole body seemed to hum with contentment as individual cells continued to sigh their pleasure.

Qadir sure knew his way around a woman's body. She felt as if she'd stepped onto a new plane of sensual pleasure and she couldn't wait to go back again.

"Not a good idea," she told herself as she stepped through the French doors and back into her room.

Last night had been amazing and fifteen kinds of a mistake. She'd been determined to hold her heart safely out of reach. Making love with Qadir for hours on end was not going to help her cause.

She couldn't get over how concerned he'd been about hurting her. He hadn't, of course, but the worry had been sweet. And the passion had been mind-altering.

"I am a mature woman," she told herself as she headed into the bathroom. "I can handle this."

She didn't have much choice. Despite how amazing the lovemaking had been, nothing had changed. She was still who she was and Qadir was still a prince.

She showered, then dried off and dressed. After combing out

her hair, she reached for the blow-dryer, but before she could turn it on, someone pounded on her door.

She moved through the living room and opened it. Victoria stood in the hallway.

"There you are," her friend said. "What is going on with you? I've been calling and calling and knocking and you haven't…" Victoria's blue eyes widened. "Oh my God. What happened?"

Maggie felt herself flush even as she said, "Nothing."

"It's not nothing. There's something totally different about you."

Was that possible? Did last night show?

"I have no idea what you're talking about," she lied.

Victoria leaned closer and stared into her eyes. "I swear, there's something. It's—" Her mouth dropped open. "No way."

The flush increased. Maggie stepped away from the open door and returned to the bathroom. "I have no idea what you're going on about."

"You are so lying. You were with Qadir last night. You were with him big-time."

As she spoke, Victoria trailed after Maggie into the bathroom. When Maggie tried to turn on the blow-dryer to drown her out, Victoria simply pulled the plug.

Maggie looked at her in the mirror. "It just happened," she admitted. "It was probably crazy, but I can't regret it."

"I want details," Victoria said. "Even more important, I'm here for you."

"I appreciate that, but I feel fine."

"You won't for long." Her friend took a deep breath. "Jon is here. He arrived in the middle of the night and he's been raising hell downstairs, trying to find you."

Maggie wished she were the kind of person who could faint on command. This seemed like an excellent time to pass out. But she stayed annoyingly conscious as Victoria led her to the private room Jon had been assigned.

"How much hell?" Maggie asked, not sure she wanted to know.

"When we couldn't find you right away, he started accusing the palace guards of holding you prisoner. They didn't know who he was or what he wanted. When he started on the 'I'm an American' rant they called me. I assured him you were fine, which he almost believed, but then I couldn't find you, either. Honestly, I never thought to check in Qadir's room. I thought you were with the car, or taking a midnight jog or something."

"I can't believe he's here," Maggie muttered. "I can't believe he's here *now*."

"At least your life isn't boring."

"I wouldn't mind boring," Maggie said, refusing to feel guilty for what had happened with Qadir. She was sorry everyone had been put out because they couldn't find her, but she had the right to a life. Jon had sure moved on. She could, too.

"I can't believe he didn't tell me he was coming," she said.

Victoria stopped in front of a door and pointed. "Good luck."

Maggie didn't want to go inside by herself. "You could come with me."

"I could, but I think you need to do this on your own." She hugged Maggie, then hurried away.

Maggie stared at the door. She had a feeling she knew why Jon had arrived in El Deharia. After last night, she would have said gathering the energy to fight was impossible, but knowing Jon as she did, she was going to have to get her mad up or he would be making all the decisions. The last thing either of them needed was a situation that would impact the rest of their lives. Of course the pregnancy had already done a good job of that.

She knocked once and the door flew open. Jon stood there, looking as he always had.

"Where have you been?" he demanded. "I got here hours ago and no one could find you. Are they keeping you hostage somewhere? What's going on here, Maggie?"

She stepped into his room, a space much smaller than her own. It faced the garden rather than the sea.

She looked at him, at the kind brown eyes, the mouth that curved into a crooked smile, the unruly brown hair he kept cut short so it didn't get too wild.

This was Jon. He'd been the boy she'd grown up with, the man she'd fallen in love with. She deliberately remembered good times they'd shared and buried herself in those memories. She dug through her heart and felt…nothing.

Until that moment she thought it was over, but she hadn't had proof. She did now. Whatever she and Jon had once shared had changed and faded until there was only a friendship she hoped would never go away.

"I'm sorry you were worried," she said. "I didn't know you were coming."

"It was a last-minute decision," he admitted.

She thought about pointing out that there were no direct flights to El Deharia. That he had to stop somewhere and he could have easily called. But he had obviously wanted to surprise her. Which he'd done.

"I'm here now." She crossed to the sofa and sat down. "Why don't you tell me why you're here."

She spoke calmly, hoping she was wrong in her assumptions.

"You're pregnant, Maggie," he said as he paced in front of her. "I'm here to bring you home. You don't belong here. You should be home. With me."

"Married to you," she clarified.

"Yes. We'll get married."

She wanted to hold on to her temper. Getting angry wouldn't help either of them.

"I'm not leaving anytime soon," she told him. "I came to El Deharia to do a job and I'm going to complete it."

He looked at her, impatience tightening his features. "It's just a car."

That really pissed her off. Her hands clenched, but still she held on to her calm. "It's my work," she corrected. "It's what I do. Prince Qadir is paying me a lot of money to restore his car and I will finish the work before I leave."

"I won't allow it."

That got her to her feet. "Fortunately it's not your decision to make."

"You're having a baby. You shouldn't be around cars."

"That's ridiculous. I'm restoring a car, not working in a toxic waste dump."

"Come home with me now."

"No."

They stared at each other, a small coffee table between them. But the distance felt much greater.

Had Jon always been like this? she wondered. Had he always tried to boss her around? Why hadn't she noticed before?

Her anger faded as sadness took its place. "This isn't what I want," she said quietly. "If nothing else, we have to stay friends."

"I'm not interested in being friends." His voice was a growl. "I'm here to marry you."

"You keep saying that and I keep telling you no." She walked around the coffee table and touched his arm. "Jon, just stop. We don't have to be like this. I'm only a few weeks pregnant. We have months ahead of us. No decisions have to be made today. I appreciate your concern, because I know what this is about. You want to do the right thing. That's the kind of man you are. But there are a lot of different right things we can do. Let's explore them. Take a breath. Go home. I'll be back in a month or so and we can figure out what we want to do."

"I want to marry you."

She held in a scream. "I don't remember you being this stubborn before."

"You were never carrying my baby before. Getting married is the right thing to do."

"Right for who? Do you really want to spend the next eighteen years tied to me? You don't love me. I appreciate that you're concerned about the baby, but how happy will this child be knowing his or her parents don't want to be married to each other?"

His stubborn expression didn't change. "We were in love before. We'll be fine."

"No, we won't. We'll be miserable. I won't do it. I won't marry you because of the child. You can't make me."

"I'm not leaving until you agree."

Maggie thought longingly of the dungeons Victoria had mentioned. "Then we have a real problem because I'll never agree."

Whatever he was going to say was lost when someone knocked on the door. Victoria stepped inside.

"I'm sorry to interrupt, but there's been another twist in your life."

She held the door open and Qadir entered, leading a young woman Maggie had never seen. She was petite, with dark blond hair and features that were probably pretty when they weren't blotchy. Tears filled the woman's eyes when she saw Jon.

"I had to come," she told him.

Elaine, Maggie thought, wondering how the situation could get worse. Then she met Qadir's gaze. What must he think of all this? Of her? Last night had been so perfect, but this morning was a disaster. Did he think she wanted to marry Jon? Was he feeling that she had simply used him?

Too many questions that she had no way to ask.

Elaine hurried over to Jon. She clutched his arm. "Don't do this," she pleaded, tears spilling down her cheeks. "Please, don't do this."

"It's the right thing for the baby."

"How is that possible? How can something that hurts this much be right?"

Maggie looked away, feeling as if she were intruding on a private moment.

"Don't you love me anymore?" Elaine asked, her voice trembling.

"Elaine, please." Jon sounded strained.

"Just tell me the truth," she pleaded. "Tell me I don't matter."

"I can't do that."

Maggie wanted to crawl into a hole. While she knew in her head she wasn't the only one to blame for the disaster, she felt the heavy weight of responsibility in her heart.

Still not looking at Jon or Elaine, she hurried out of the room and into the hallway.

Someone came after her. She half expected it to be Victoria, but then she felt strong hands settle on her shoulders.

"Who needs daytime television when they can just watch what's going on in my life," she said, trying to make light of the situation.

Qadir turned her to face him, then pulled her close.

"I can't believe this is happening," she said as she snuggled into his chest. "I can't believe Jon is here and Elaine followed him. He wants to marry me."

"I expected no less. If you were carrying my child, I would not let you get away."

Words to make her tremble, she thought sadly. If she were carrying Qadir's child, she wouldn't want to get away.

"I'm not going to ruin all our lives because I'm pregnant. You saw Elaine. She loves him desperately. He's wrong to push for a marriage with me."

"He's a man who is trying to do the right thing. His conscience wars with his heart."

"His heart better win."

Victoria slipped into the hallway. "I'm going to find Elaine a room. Apparently she's staying, at least for now."

Maggie winced. "Here? That can't be okay. We should all move to a hotel."

"The palace has many rooms," Qadir told her. "Your friends are welcome."

They weren't her friends, but there was no point in getting into that. And she sure didn't want to think what the staff must be thinking about her.

"This is all my fault."

Qadir touched her cheek. "It is not."

Elaine came out of the room and looked at Maggie. "He wants to talk to you."

Maggie nodded. "I'm sorry. I didn't want any of this to happen."

"I believe you. I wish things were different."

Victoria led the other woman away. Maggie stared at the half-open door. "I guess I need to go back inside."

"I will come with you," Qadir said.

"No, that's okay. I can handle Jon."

Qadir hesitated, as if he wasn't going to give her a choice. Then he nodded. "If there is any trouble, you will get in touch with me."

It wasn't a question.

"I promise," she told him.

He bent his head and brushed his mouth against hers, then walked away. Maggie braced herself and walked into Jon's room.

He stood by the window, looking out onto the garden. His

body was stiff, but his shoulders seemed bowed, as if they carried too heavy a weight.

"I didn't know Elaine would follow me," he said without turning around. "I'm sorry about that."

"I'm impressed. She obviously loves you very much and isn't willing to let you get away."

"She doesn't understand."

"She understands perfectly." Maggie waited until he turned to face her before continuing. "She understands that you're willing to throw away everything important to you for no good reason. She understands that while no one would have chosen this situation, it's here now and we have to deal with it. But what she doesn't understand—and I have to say I'm with her on that—is why you think there's only one option."

"Because there is. There's the right thing to do and there's everything else."

Had he always been this stubborn? "Is it because I suggested you give up the child altogether?" she asked. "Did that make you feel like I was cutting you out and pushing you away? Is that why you're so insistent?"

He didn't say anything and she couldn't read him anymore. Their intimate connection had been broken.

"I'm sorry," she said. "I shouldn't have gone there. Maybe it is the right thing for both of us, but it was wrong of me to assume anything. We need to come to a decision together. Maybe the three of us should talk."

"This doesn't involve Elaine."

"Of course it does. It's her future, too. Her life. Chances are, she's going to be a stepmother."

"You and I are the ones getting married."

Maggie rolled her eyes. "Listen to me very, very carefully. I will not marry you and you can't make me. I don't love you. You don't love me. In fact, you're in love with someone else. Now quit being an idiot and start looking at other alternatives."

"No."

"Then rot in this room. I'm done talking to you. When you're ready to be rational and reasonable, come find me. Otherwise, I don't want to see you again."

By seven that night, Maggie had a pounding headache and a deep desire to ride into the desert and never be heard from again. She sat alone in her room wondering how on earth she was supposed to fix the disaster that was her life.

She heard a light tapping on her French door. When she stood, she saw Victoria standing there with a pint of ice cream in each hand. Maggie hurried to let her in.

"I'm sneaking around," her friend admitted, holding out the cartons. "I don't want to see anyone or talk to anyone. Except you, I guess. Which one do you want?"

Maggie grabbed one of the cartons without checking the flavor, then frowned. "What's wrong?"

Victoria's blue eyes were swollen and red, her mouth puffy. "I've been crying. Me and Elaine. It's our day. Neither of us seem to be pretty criers. I'm hoping you won't be judgmental."

"Of course not. But what's wrong?"

"Nothing. Everything. It's so stupid. It's not like I really care. It's just I had this plan, you know. Then I tell myself I never thought it would happen, so what's the big deal? I mean, who am I kidding? A prince? Marry me?"

Maggie led her to the sofa and urged her to sit. "I have no idea what you're talking about."

Victoria scooped out some ice cream and licked the spoon. "I hope you appreciate that my escape of choice would be margaritas. But I hate to drink by myself and you're pregnant, so I'm stuck with ice cream."

"Still confused."

She sniffed again. "Nadim is engaged. His father found him a perfectly nice young woman. She comes from a respectable family with little in the way of financial success, but the lineage is impressive enough on its own. They apparently met last week, spent the weekend away to determine if they were compatible. All went well and now they're engaged."

Tears filled her eyes. "I know it's ridiculous. Who wants to be with a man who is that emotionally disconnected? He can't know if he likes her or not after a damn weekend. It's just I had this silly dream, you know? One where I could be financially secure and not have to worry, like I did when I was growing up. But who am I kidding? Stuff like that doesn't happen to women like me."

Maggie didn't know enough about Victoria's past to know what she was talking about. She only knew that her friend was in pain.

"Nadim is really engaged?"

"They're going to make the announcement in a couple of weeks, after As'ad and Kayleen's wedding. They don't want to take away from the happy event." She wiped her face with the back of her hand. "He didn't even tell me directly. I found out because he gave me some letters to type and they mentioned his engagement. He doesn't even know I'm alive."

"Then he's not worth even one of your tears," Maggie said. "Come on. You didn't love him. I'm not even sure you liked him."

"It wasn't about liking. It was about being safe."

"You are safe. You have a great job, you live in a palace."

"Until I get fired."

"Why would Nadim fire you? Don't you do a good job?"

"Yes."

"You have savings?"

"Uh-huh. I'm a big saver."

"So you're okay. Nadim was never the man for you. Maybe it's time to go out and live life."

"No, thanks. Life hurts." She jabbed at her ice cream. "I suppose the bright side is at least you got a proposal today."

"From someone I don't want to marry."

"It's the thought that counts," Victoria said, then started to laugh.

Maggie joined in. The two of them leaned back on the sofa and laughed until they started crying, then they tuned the TV to a shopping channel, leaned back and ate their ice cream.

Chapter Twelve

Jon showed up in the garage the next morning. Maggie put down her tools, knowing whatever he had to say, she had to listen, then convince him why he was wrong.

"You've been avoiding me," he said.

"Under the circumstances, it seemed the smart thing to do."

"You don't want to marry me."

She wasn't ready for relief. She couldn't tell if he'd really gotten it or was just testing her. "I don't want to marry you."

Jon shoved his hands into his pockets and walked around the car. "I talked to Elaine last night. All night. She pointed out I can't force you to. Even if I could, it would only lead to disaster."

Maggie had a feeling she was going to like Elaine. "I have to take a lot of the blame," she said. "I should never have mentioned you walking away from the child. That's not who you are. I'm going to guess that made you think I planned to shut you out, which you reacted to."

"I didn't like it," he told her. "This is my child, too."

"I know. I'm sorry."

"It's okay." He looked at the car. "It's not much to look at now, but you're going to make it beautiful."

"That's the plan."

"We went out to dinner. The city seems nice."

"I like it."

He stopped in front of her. "I love her," he said with a shrug. "I really love her. It's different, Mags. I can't explain how it's different, but it is. I want to be with her every second. I think about her when we're apart. It's exciting and new, but it's also comfortable. We're the same in ways you and I never were. I love her and I want to be with her always."

Maggie swallowed. "I'm happy for you," she said, and meant it. The only hint of pain came from the voice inside that said she would like that, too. Not with Jon, of course, but with someone.

She thought of Qadir and how the handsome prince had stolen a piece of her heart. The problem wasn't her feelings for him but his for her. Did he have any? Things had changed for her but she had a bad feeling they were exactly the same for him.

"I won't cut you out of the baby's life. I swear. If that's not good enough, and I understand it might not be, then I'll sign something. We'll figure out a plan. You can have summers or weekends or whatever works best. But don't lose the love of your life over this."

"You're right," he said, words she couldn't ever remember him speaking.

"I know I'm right," she teased, to keep the mood light. "Now go find your woman and take her until she's boneless. Then tell her you're sorry and that she's the one you really want to marry."

"I will," he said, and hugged her.

She stepped into his embrace. Everything about it was familiar but none of it was what she wanted.

"If you need anything, I'll be there for you," he said when he released her.

"I know." She stepped back and smiled at him. "Thanks for being willing to do the right thing. Even if it was totally crazy."

He smiled. "You have to admit, I have style."

"Oh, yeah. Now go find Elaine and tell her she owes me."

"Love you, Mags."

She believed he did love her, the way she loved him. Like an old friend. Jon was a warm memory from her past and she would never forget him. But he wasn't the one.

"I love you, too."

She watched him walk away. Elaine would be waiting, praying that she wasn't about to lose the man of her dreams. They would talk and kiss and make love. If Jon was smart, he would propose and they would fly home blissfully happy. It was what Maggie wanted for them. She sure didn't want Jon for herself. But that didn't make her feel any less alone.

Maggie spent the day feeling restless. She gave up working on the car early in the afternoon and went for a walk in the garden.

There were hundreds of different plants, trees and shrubs and she doubted she knew the names of any of them. Still, their beauty calmed her spirit and the perfume of their combined scents helped her relax.

She walked along the various paths, taking turns she never had before. She found herself next to a high wall. A soft cry came from behind the stone. Someone was in trouble!

"It is not what you think."

She turned and found Qadir standing behind her. Her reaction was, as always, instant and powerful. She gave in to the need and rushed into his arms.

He held her tightly against him, rubbing his hands up and down her back. "Fear not," he told her. "I am here. I will slay your dragons."

If only that were true, she thought as she held on, never wanting to let go. "I'm sort of dragon free right now," she told him.

"Should that change, my sword is at your disposal."

She stepped back and looked at him. "You have a sword?"

He raised his eyebrows, which made her laugh.

"Not that," she said with a smile. "Do you have a real sword? You know, made of metal and all sharp and shiny."

"Of course."

"Then I'll let you know the next time I see a dragon."

He took her hand in his and led her closer to the wall. "The crying is not what you think."

"It sounds like a kitten is lost inside. Or someone is in trouble."

"Sometimes it sounds like a child. Instead there are two old parrots. The last of them. These walls hide the harem garden. Many years ago, when my great-grandfather kept women here, parrots lived in the garden. Their cries concealed the voices of the women so no man would be tempted to climb the walls and claim what could never be his."

She stared at him. "There was a harem here?"

"Of course."

"Women kept against their will?"

"Dozens of the most beautiful women in the world."

"That's disgusting."

"Not for the king."

She glared at him. "Don't you dare become a sexist pig. I swear, I'll stab you in your sleep."

"Pregnancy has made you violent."

"Maybe I've always been this way."

"Perhaps." He leaned down and kissed her nose. "You need a good taming. Time in a harem would do that."

"I'm not really harem material. I would rebel and escape."

"Perhaps your master would so satisfy you that you would not want to be anywhere else."

The way Qadir had satisfied her? "I'm not the type who takes to confinement well."

"I would agree. You are far too independent."

For a harem or for him?

She told herself that she was only making herself crazy. Qadir had never hinted he wanted anything but the bargain they'd agreed upon. The fact that her feelings were changing didn't shift reality. She supposed the only question she had to deal with was whether or not she could stay and pretend to be involved with him when, for her at least, it was no longer a game.

"I'm glad there isn't a harem anymore," she said. "Knowing there were women locked up would really annoy me."

"I am not so sure. At times I miss the old ways."

She looked at him and saw the humor in his eyes. "You're really flirting with danger here. Just because you're a prince doesn't mean I can't take you."

"You cannot take me. Not in the way you mean. But there are other ways to bring me to my knees, Maggie, and those you know well."

His words made her tremble, then step closer so they could kiss.

His mouth was firm without being hard, offering as much as it took. She kissed him back with a passion that burned so hot she knew she would carry the scars forever.

When he led her back toward the palace, she went with him.

Yes, there was a risk in being with Qadir over and over. But she would face the pain later. For now, building memories would have to be enough.

"I love weddings," Victoria said as they walked along the hallway. "Which is strange when you think about it. I'm so opposed to love. But I guess I don't mind other people making emotional fools out of themselves."

"You're such a romantic," Maggie teased, wishing they weren't going so fast. She still wasn't comfortable walking in high heels.

Although As'ad and Kayleen's wedding was in the morning, it was still a dressy affair.

"Thanks for helping me get ready," Maggie said as she smoothed the front of her dress.

"No problem. I loved playing dress-up as a kid. You look beautiful, which is important. There will be lots of press hanging around. They won't be allowed in the ceremony, of course, but expect to have your picture taken."

Not an exciting thought, Maggie told herself. "I guess a small, intimate wedding just for family is out of the question."

"When the man you're marrying is a prince, then yes. By royal standards, this is small. There are also different traditions. No attendants. While As'ad's brothers will sit up front, they won't stand with him." Victoria smiled at her. "Which explains why you'll be there with Qadir and I'll be in the back with the other rabble."

"I'd rather sit with you," Maggie said earnestly. At least with Victoria, she wouldn't feel like a fraud.

"You'll be fine. There's really nothing to do but smile and be happy for the lucky couple. Don't worry. I'll watch all the famous people coming in, then catch up with you at the reception and let you know what movie stars are here. There will also be the usual foreign dignitaries, which is less interesting. They even got Kateb, the mystery brother, to come in from the desert for the event."

Maggie looked at her friend. "I've met him. He seems nice."

Victoria shook her head. "I don't think anyone has ever used that word to describe him. He's dark and mysterious. A man of the desert, which means he's ruled by emotions. Too passionate for me. Give me a prince like Nadim who doesn't know how to feel. Kateb is nothing but trouble."

Victoria sighed. "Not that it's an issue anymore. I'm giving up on princes."

"Really?"

"Uh-huh. I thought about what you said before. I can take care of myself. I'm well paid working here and I don't have any expenses except for clothes and vacations. I've done some traveling but always on the cheap and you've seen where I shop. I guess you can take the girl out of poverty but you can't take poverty out of the girl. Anyway, I have a fairly big savings account. I've decided to come up with a new plan."

"Which is?"

"I'm going to work here another year and keep saving, then I'm going back to the States and opening my own business. I don't know what it will be yet, but I have time to figure it out. I don't need a prince to be happy. I can avoid men at home just as easily as I have here."

"Good for you," Maggie said, not sure it was good. Having Victoria recognize that she was capable of taking care of herself was excellent, but cutting herself off emotionally wasn't exactly healthy. "And you might meet someone nice."

"No, thanks. I have no interest in getting married for the sake of it. With Nadim, I was looking for security. Now that I don't need that, I'm going to avoid men. All men."

They walked down the stairs to the main level and heard the crowd of waiting guests before they saw them. Victoria pointed toward a side door.

"Go through there. You'll find Qadir and the rest of the wedding party. I'll see you at the reception."

Maggie opened her mouth to protest that she wanted to stay with her friend, but Victoria gave her a little push. Maggie walked toward the door, then opened it and went through.

Members of the royal family were gathered around. Maggie recognized a few of them, while others were unfamiliar. She saw Qadir's aunt who was now Queen of Bahania, along with Qadir's brothers. The king was there, as well.

She circled the room, avoiding the monarch, looking for Qadir. Maybe she could explain it would be easier for everyone if she simply sat with Victoria.

A servant walked by with a tray of champagne. She shook her head as she eased back into a corner. Seconds later Qadir found her.

"Why are you hiding?" he asked by way of greeting.

"I'm not hiding, exactly." She looked around. "I don't belong here. I'm a fraud."

"Perhaps, but you are my fraud."

"You're not taking this seriously."

"Because you are taking it too seriously." He picked up her hand and kissed her knuckles. "You look beautiful. Elegant and unapproachable. Yet I know the woman inside, the one who cries out my name."

She cleared her throat. "Yes, well, that woman is busy today. I'm here in her place."

"I find this one charming, as well."

"Good to know." She looked around. "I've never been to a royal wedding before."

"They are much like others you have attended. Long and filled with tradition."

Would his wedding be like this? she wondered. When he finally found the woman he wanted to marry? Speaking of which…

"Jon and Elaine have left," she told him.

"I had heard that. All is well?"

She nodded. "They're still together and in love. Jon and I haven't figured out what we're going to do about the baby, but he no longer thinks we have to get married. We'll figure out the details later. Maybe weekends or summers. At least that's what we discussed. I was wrong to suggest he give up his child. I think that freaked him out. He reacted in the only way he knew how."

Kateb approached. "Ms. Collins, how nice to see you again."

Qadir frowned. "How do you know Maggie?"

"We met in the garden," she told him.

"I am not sure I approve."

What was it with these imperious men? "I'm not sure I care about your approval."

Kateb laughed. "It is too bad you are not involved with this one," he told his brother. "She has much to recommend herself."

Maggie knew Kateb meant his words as a compliment, but they still cut through her. The reminder that this was all a game to Qadir hurt more than it should. Not that she was surprised to be the only one who had fallen in love.

The orchestra had come from London, the flowers had been flown in from around the world. The church itself, a cathedral built in the 1600s, seated at least six hundred. Maggie sat next to Qadir in a hand-carved pew that dated back over five hundred years.

While she wouldn't want to admit it to anyone, she'd imagined her own wedding many times. For years she'd assumed she would marry Jon in a short ceremony, with her father giving her away and people she'd known all her life around them. She'd wanted a summer wedding so the days were long and the nights warm. She'd wanted to dance until she was exhausted, then drive to a secluded cabin in the woods for a week-long honeymoon.

Simple dreams, she thought now as they rose in anticipation of Kayleen walking down the rose-petal-covered aisle. Dreams that had been altered by so many unexpected turns. The loss of her father. The ending of her relationship with Jon and now falling in love with Qadir.

She might be foolish enough to fall for him, but she wasn't stupid enough to think anything would come of it. The prince and the mechanic? Who thought that was possible?

She looked down at the dress she wore. It was beautiful and expensive. Nothing she would have picked for herself. It was part of the role she played, as Qadir's girlfriend. But it wasn't who she was. She was Maggie Collins, who wore jeans and didn't bother with makeup and expected an ordinary life.

But what happened when a regular woman fell in love with an extraordinary man? How could she find happiness?

Under different circumstances she might have tried to talk herself into making things real with Qadir. But he was in line to the El Deharian throne and she was pregnant with another man's child. What was the point in telling him the truth? He would only pity her.

The first of the three girls Kayleen and As'ad had adopted stepped into view. The girls were pretty and obviously thrilled to be a part of the ceremony. They walked slowly, one after the other. Then the bride entered the church. A veil covered her face, but it was sheer enough for Maggie to see the love shining in her eyes. A radiant bride, she thought. Love made everyone beautiful.

Kayleen continued down the aisle, where an equally smitten As'ad waited.

Maggie's heart ached. She wanted this for herself. Not the fancy wedding, but the love. She wanted someone to love her forever, to hold her and never let her go.

She glanced at Qadir. She couldn't find that with him, but was it possible with someone else? The congregation sat. Qadir reached over and took her hand in his.

It was just for show, she told herself, even as she desperately wanted it to be real. Just a game. A game that was going to break her heart into so many pieces, she was unlikely to ever find a way to make herself whole again.

Maggie sanded the fender with a piece of fine sandpaper. She wanted the finish perfect, which meant doing the details herself. The work was tedious, but she didn't mind. Focusing on the car was a kind of mental vacation from the weirdness of her life these days.

She adjusted the mask she wore, wishing it weren't so hot. But she didn't want to risk breathing in any of the particles. Not while she was pregnant.

The things I do for you, kid, she thought with a smile.

Someone tapped her arm. She jumped and turned, then jerked off the mask as she recognized King Mukhtar.

"Your Highness," she said in surprise, setting down the sandpaper and wiping her hands on her coveralls. "I didn't hear you come in."

What was she supposed to do? Bow? Curtsy? Offer to shake hands?

"Stealth is important for a monarch," he said without smiling. "Might I have a moment of your time, Ms. Collins?"

That didn't sound good, she thought grimly. "Yes, of course. My office is through here."

She led the way and motioned to a seat. But the king remained standing so she did, as well.

"I will get right to the point," he said, gazing directly into her eyes. "It is time for you to leave El Deharia. You are far too pretty a distraction for my son."

Maggie didn't know what to say. The king's attitude wasn't a surprise, but she didn't think he would be so blunt.

Mukhtar continued before she could think of how to respond.

"I didn't object to the relationship initially," he told her. "Times are changing and fresh blood is always a good thing. It is not as if there are an excess of princesses or duchesses around for my sons to marry. While your circumstances are modest, so are Kayleen's and she is an excellent match for As'ad. However, recent changes in your circumstances have convinced me you are not suitable for Qadir."

Maggie stiffened, but didn't back down. He was talking about her pregnancy. She doubted anyone expected a virgin bride, but she'd gone a little to far over the line.

"Qadir needs to be available to find someone suitable. He will not look as long as you are around. Perhaps this sounds harsh to you. Unfortunately I have more to consider than most fathers. I have a country and a responsibility to my people. As does Qadir."

She'd been willing to offer a protest right up until that last bit. But how was she supposed to ignore the needs of an entire country? The king was right—she didn't belong.

"I will not ask you to pack your bags immediately," he told her. "But I would like you to begin making arrangements."

Maggie found her voice. "I have another three weeks' worth of work on the car," she said. "I don't need to stay to see it finished, but I have a few more things I must do. I'll stay through the end of the week."

"Thank you for understanding. It is most unfortunate.

Under other circumstances…" He cleared his throat. "I wish you well, child."

The king left.

Maggie stared after him. Her nature was to stand up for herself, to fight for what she wanted. But how could she? The king had told the truth. She wasn't right for Qadir and she didn't belong here. It was time for her to leave.

Chapter Thirteen

"He is an impossible old man," Qadir said as he paced the length of his living room. "Impossible."

"Agreed." Kateb lounged on one of the sofas, smoking a cigar. "Unfortunately he is the king."

"Perhaps, but he has no right to interfere."

"You are his son."

"A matter of no consequence," Qadir muttered.

Kateb merely raised his eyebrows.

"It is not his place to say who is to be in my life," Qadir continued.

"You have much energy over a matter that is very small," his brother pointed out. "Maggie was merely a convenience. You hired her to act as your girlfriend, Qadir. You were not actually with her. Why are you so angry at our father's interference?"

Qadir couldn't answer. "It is the principle of the matter," he said at last.

"Ah, well then. You must do as you see fit. But to me, the simpler solution is to let her go and find another woman to hire. What do you care who plays your pretend lover? Isn't one woman as good as the next?"

Qadir turned on his brother. The need to strike out, to punish, was as powerful as it was unexpected. Kateb studied him through a cloud of smoke, his dark gaze deceptively lazy.

"I do not want another woman," Qadir said. "Maggie suits me." She understood him. She was easy to talk to. Why would he want to start over with someone else? "She is the only one I want."

Kateb nodded slowly. "That is more of a problem."

"You will not leave," Qadir said imperiously.

Maggie was more than ready to stop being dictated to by men. First Jon, then the king and now Qadir. Of all of them, only the king made her nervous, probably because she didn't actually know how much power he had. There were still rumors of a dungeon downstairs—a place she didn't ever want to see.

"Your father wants me gone," she said as she sat on the edge of the sofa and resisted the need to bury her face in her hands. "What does it matter? Someone else can finish the car."

"You care so little for your work?"

"No, but in the scheme of things it matters a whole lot less than it did before. I've done most of the hard stuff. I'm staying through the end of the week, then I need to go." She drew in a breath. "Qadir, I know you had your plan all worked out, but it isn't going to work. Not with me." She hated saying that, but it was true.

"The reality is, you can hire someone else," she continued. "Someone who isn't pregnant." Maybe someone who would be smart enough not to fall in love with him.

She couldn't think about that, she reminded herself. That was her vow. That she wouldn't allow herself to get into her feelings until she was safely on a plane back to Aspen. Then she would have a small but tasteful breakdown and really feel the pain. It would probably frighten the other people on the flight, but they would have to deal with that.

"I do not want someone else. I want you."

His words settled on her like a warm, cozy blanket. She held them close, hardly able to believe that he was actually—

"You are easy to talk to. We share a sense of humor and excellent chemistry. I am unlikely to find that again and it will not be convenient for me to look."

She leaned back against the sofa and closed her eyes. Not only did he know where to slide in the knife, he knew exactly how to twist it for maximum effect.

Not that she should blame him. Qadir had no clue as to her real feelings so he couldn't know how he was hurting her.

"Qadir, I really think that I—"

"I have decided there is only one solution," he said, interrupting her. "We will be married."

Maggie sat up. "Excuse me?"

"We will be married. My father wants me to be married and I have no interest in someone he will thrust upon me. As I have stated, you and I get along well. I understand this match will have many advantages for you, which is also a good thing. It will be more difficult for Jon to see his child regularly, but you mentioned he could have the child for summers and I would not object to that."

"I… You…" She stared at him, too stunned to form sentences.

"It is a great honor," Qadir said kindly. "You are surprised at my generosity. I am confident we will both be happy in this marriage. While my father may take a while to convince, he will be pleased that you are a known breeder."

Her brain was blank. Totally blank. Which was probably a good thing because if she had actual use of her functions, she would be forced to hit him over the head with a lamp.

"A known breeder?" she ground out.

He smiled. "That was meant to be humorous," he told her. "What do you say, Maggie? It is an excellent solution for both of us."

"Solution? To what problem? You're the one who has to get married, not me. No one is pressuring me to take a husband."

She hurt all over. She *loved* him. She could imagine nothing more amazing than having him say he cared about her and wanted to be with her always. But that was just a fantasy. The reality was Qadir wasn't interested in being emotionally connected to anyone. He wanted a companion he liked and someone to have great sex with.

"Why are you angry?" he asked. Damn him, he actually looked confused. "I am doing you a great honor. I am Prince Qadir of El Deharia, Maggie. You would be my princess. A member of the royal family. Your children with me would be part of our history."

"Not bad for a car mechanic from Colorado, right?" she said bitterly, then held up her hands. "Never mind answering. I know you don't get it. Most of the time you're almost a regular guy. I started to forget the whole prince thing. But that's a part of you, too."

His gaze narrowed. "Are you saying that is something you do not like?"

"It's not my favorite characteristic."

Too late she remembered his ex-fiancée, Whitney, who wouldn't marry him because she didn't want to deal with the restrictions of being a princess.

"It's not just that," she said quickly. "I'm not going to marry you to better my financial situation. That's not who I am. And I'm not going to marry you because it's convenient. I wouldn't marry Jon and he thought he was doing the right thing."

"Do not compare me to him."

"Why not? You're both interested in getting me to marry you for reasons that have nothing to do with me and everything to do with yourselves. That's not what I want."

She hurt all over. Her chest ached when she breathed and she just wanted to be alone.

She stood and walked to the door. After pulling it open, she shook her head. "Look. I know you think you're doing me this big favor, but I don't see it that way. I want something different. Something you can't give me. And I'm not going to settle for anything less." She opened the door a little wider. "You should go now."

Maggie lay curled up on the bed, crying so hard, her whole body shook. She knew she should stop, that this much emotion couldn't be good for the baby, but she didn't know how.

"It's all right," Victoria said, stroking her back. "I'll go online and find someone to beat the crap out of Qadir. That will help."

"Not much."

"But a little. Right?"

Maggie reached for another tissue and blew her nose. "I can't believe he did that. I can't believe he proposed that way. What was he thinking?"

"He wasn't. I have no idea. Men can be really, really stupid. Even princes."

"Especially princes. He told me it would be an honor for me to marry him."

"What a jerk."

Maggie nodded and looked at her friend. "I love him."

Victoria gave her a sad smile. "I figured that out. Unfortunately he didn't."

"I don't want him to know. Then he'd only pity me. It's better that he doesn't understand me. At least that's what I keep telling myself." More tears filled her eyes. "I just don't know how to get through this."

"One second at a time. You keep breathing, keep putting one foot in front of the other."

"I want to go home. I have a doctor's appointment tomorrow. I want to make sure it's okay for me to fly with the baby and all, and then I'm gone."

"I'll miss you," Victoria said.

"You're leaving soon, too, aren't you? Come to Aspen. It's beautiful and there are lots of rich, powerful men hanging around the slopes."

"I'm done with rich, powerful men but I will come visit you. I want to be there when the baby is born."

"I'd like that." Otherwise Maggie would be alone. She knew Jon would offer to be with her, but that would be too weird.

At least he could be talked out of it. Qadir would not. He would storm into the delivery room and demand to be a part of things. She started to cry again.

"I wish I didn't love him," she said. "I didn't want it to be like this. I didn't want to be one of those women crushed by a man."

"You're not."

"Look at me."

"You'll get over this and be stronger for it."

Maggie didn't believe her. "Why couldn't he love me?"

"Men like him don't fall in love," Victoria told her. "They take what's offered and move on. They don't have to give their hearts. It's never required of them."

Maggie wanted to disagree and say Qadir wasn't like that, only he was. After all, he'd been the one to come up with the idea of them pretending to be involved. He was also willing to marry her even though he didn't love her.

"I want a man who loves me passionately," she whispered. "I want to matter more than anything."

"Not me," Victoria told her. "Love is messy."

Right now messy looked pretty good.

"Tell me the pain will get better," she said.

"You know it will. You're going to heal and move on. One day you'll look back on all this and be grateful you got away when you did."

Maggie hoped her friend was right, but she had her doubts.

The doctor's office was in a modern building next to a hospital. Maggie showed up a few minutes early for her appointment to fill out paperwork.

Victoria had found the female doctor by asking around at the palace and then had even phoned to make the appointment. Maggie was going to miss her when she left.

After checking in for her appointment, she took the clipboard over to one of the comfortable seats and began filling in the information. She hesitated at the line that asked for her home address, then wrote in that of the palace.

In a few days that wouldn't be true anymore. She already had her ticket home to Aspen. Once there, she would find an apartment to rent until she got her house back, then start looking for a job. She would have to put away as much money as possible before the baby came.

She answered all the health questions. She had no symptoms of anything unusual and so far, no problems with her pregnancy. Still, a part of her hoped to be told she couldn't fly for a few more weeks. Which was just dumb. What did she think? That more time would make Qadir realize he was madly in love with her? Like that was ever going to happen.

With the paperwork completed and turned in, she flipped through a magazine before she was called in to the exam room.

Dr. Galloway was a friendly woman in her late forties. They discussed her due date, prenatal vitamins and Maggie's new dietary needs.

"While everyone wants to eat for two," Dr. Galloway told her, "you're currently eating for yourself and something the size of a rice grain. It's better for you and the baby if you can keep your weight down. The more you put on now, the more you'll have to take off later."

"I'll keep that in mind," Maggie said, knowing lately she was too sad to eat. She would have to force herself to stay healthy for the sake of the baby. "Is it all right for me to fly?"

"Sure. There aren't any problems in the first few months."

"Thanks." Maggie tried not to sound disappointed. It appeared there was nothing keeping her in El Deharia.

The doctor smiled at her. "It's a little early, so I can't promise, but would you like to try to hear the baby's heartbeat?"

"Yes. Of course."

"We'll get set up in a—"

There was a commotion in the hall, the sound of footsteps followed by a woman saying, "You can't go in there. Sir, you can't."

"I am Prince Qadir. I may go where I like."

"Sir, there are *patients*."

"Then tell me where she is."

Dr. Galloway rose. "What on earth is that?"

Maggie sat up. "Um, he's with me."

The doctor stared at her. "He's the—"

"No. Not the father. Just someone I know. He's..." She

shrugged, not sure how to explain about Qadir's imperious proposal and impossible assumptions.

"You can let him in," Maggie said. "It's okay."

Dr. Galloway left to get Qadir while Maggie tried to figure out what he was doing at the doctor's office. How had he even known about her appointment? Then she remembered the date book on her desk. Had he looked there?

She knew better than to be happy about the invasion. Qadir was here for his own reasons, but they were unlikely to be overly thrilling to her.

The door to the exam room flew open and he stalked inside. "You did not tell me about your appointment."

"I know."

"I wish to be informed of these things."

"Why?"

"Because it is not right for you to keep this information from me."

She sat up on the examining table and did her best to look dignified while dressed in a thin cloth gown that tied in the back.

"This isn't your child," she reminded him, refusing to get lost in his dark eyes or remember how good his mouth felt against hers. "You have nothing to do with my pregnancy."

"I want to marry you and be a father to your child. That makes me involved."

"I didn't accept your proposal. Weren't you listening?"

"You weren't saying anything I wanted to hear." He reached for her hand. "Maggie, why are you being difficult?"

She snatched her fingers away before he could touch them. "This isn't difficult, Qadir, it's real. I'm not willing to be a convenience in your life. I want more."

The door opened and a young woman wheeled in a monitor. She paused. "Should I come back?"

"Yes," Qadir said impatiently.

"No," Maggie told her as she scowled at him. "I want her to stay. I might be able to hear the baby's heartbeat."

His expression softened. "So soon?"

"We can try," the technician told him.

"I would like to stay and listen."

Maggie thought about fighting him, but what was the point?

She lay back down and was hooked up to the monitor. A few minutes later, a soft, steady beating filled the room.

It was the most beautiful sound she'd ever heard and it terrified her to the bone. There really was a baby. She was going to be a mother and responsible for the life growing inside her.

What if she wasn't any good? What if she messed everything up? Then she remembered her father and how much he'd loved her. She wanted that for herself and her child.

She turned to look at Qadir, to see if he understood the wonder of the moment and was crushed to find he had slipped out when she wasn't paying attention. Apparently he hadn't cared as much as he claimed.

"It was the sound," Qadir said as he once again paced, but this time in his brother's quarters.

"A heartbeat?" Kateb sounded unimpressed.

"Yes, but more than that. I cannot explain what it was like. There in the room. Proof of life."

"You know this isn't your child," Kateb said.

Qadir dismissed the information. "Not the child of my body, but we are still connected. I will forbid her to leave. It is within my power."

"Not without reason," his brother reminded him. "You could always drag her into the desert. I know places where you will never be found."

"Maggie would not enjoy the desert," Qadir said, wondering why she had to be so difficult and how he could convince her she had to stay. "There must be something I am not saying to her. Something she wants to hear."

His brother looked at him. "You're not serious, are you?"

"What?"

"You really don't understand why she's not happy with you?"

"And you do?"

Kateb stood and faced him. "She's a woman. She wants to be loved."

Qadir stiffened. "No. I will not."

"Because you loved Whitney and she walked away?"

Qadir ignored the question. He would not speak of her with his brother. The pain was too—

He paused. There was no pain. Whitney had been many years ago. Perhaps she was the reason he was reluctant to fully engage his heart, but he no longer cared for her in any way. But to risk loving again…

"Whitney didn't stay because she couldn't face what being your wife meant," Kateb said. "Is that Maggie's problem?"

"No. She is fearless." Feisty and determined. She challenged him. He enjoyed her challenges, especially in bed.

"So the problem seems to be you."

Qadir glared. "I have proposed. She has refused. The problem is hers."

"Did you tell her you love her?"

"No."

"Did it ever occur to you that you should?"

He started to explain to his brother that the problem was he didn't love Maggie, but he couldn't seem to speak the words. Why was that?

Did he love her? Was that why he'd wanted to grind Jon into the dust? Why he didn't want to let her go?

"I do love her," he announced. "I love Maggie."

Kateb smirked. "Then you should probably go and tell her."

Maggie left the palace in a cab. She supposed she could have gotten one of the limo drivers to take her, but somehow that didn't seem right.

She had the driver wait for a few minutes, hoping Victoria would show up to say goodbye, but she did not. Her friend had disappeared, leaving only a note saying her father had unexpectedly arrived and that she would try to stop by if she could.

Finally Maggie got in the cab and they drove away.

She stared out at the passing city, trying to take in the beauty of it all. Anything to keep her mind off her sadness. She'd come to El Deharia with high hopes and was leaving with a broken heart. She would miss her friend. Even more, she would miss the man she loved.

Alone, near tears, she admitted to herself that she had hoped he would at least try to talk her into staying. She'd hoped for one more annoying conversation where he told her what to do and she refused. At least then she could see him one more time. But he hadn't bothered.

She told herself she would get over him, even as a part of her knew that she was going to love him forever. Eventually she might be able to find a man she could like a lot, but the arrogant prince would always have her heart. Unfortunately he was too stupid to appreciate that.

Once at the busy airport, she paid the driver and walked into the terminal. She stood in line to check in. When it was her turn, the clerk took her electronic ticket and her passport and typed into the computer. The young woman frowned.

"What's wrong?" Maggie asked.

"There seems to be a problem, Ms. Collins. I'm going to have to ask you to speak with one of our security officers."

"What?"

Before she could find out what was going on, she was whisked into a small room with a single desk, two chairs and no windows. An official-looking little man stacked her luggage in the corner before facing her.

"Ms. Collins, I'm very sorry, but I'm going to have to arrest you."

This couldn't be happening, Maggie thought. It was a joke. It had to be.

"For what?"

"Violating El Deharian law. You are pregnant?"

"That has nothing to do with anything."

"I'll take that as a yes. It is illegal to remove a royal child from the country without permission from the king. You have no such permission."

She sank into the chair. Disbelief warred with despair. Wasn't her life sucky enough without this happening?

"The baby isn't Qadir's," she said, not looking at the little man. "I know what the papers said, but they're wrong. If you would just call him, he'll tell you that and you can let me go."

"That is the one thing I cannot do."

That voice!

Maggie stood and saw Qadir had entered the small room. He walked to her and took her hands in his as the security agent left.

She didn't know what to think. "Why are you here?"

"Because you left before I could speak with you. Because if you leave, I will only follow and that will make us both look foolish."

His dark gaze burned down to her soul. "Maggie, I have realized what is wrong. Why you won't stay and marry me."

"I doubt that."

He smiled. "You are difficult and stubborn and I never wish to tame you."

"I'm fairly untamable."

"Even for the man who loves you?"

Time froze. She couldn't breathe, couldn't speak, could only stare into Qadir's face.

"I love you," he said firmly. "I want you to stay so we can be together. I want you to stay so I can be a father to your child. I want you to stay because we belong together. Be my wife."

The words were magic but a little surprising. "Have you had a recent head injury?"

Qadir laughed, then pulled her close and kissed her. "I have been a fool. Many years ago, I gave my heart. When it was broken, I vowed to never love again. I did not recognize what had happened until it was almost too late."

Joy filled her until she thought she might float. She flung herself at him and held on as hard as she could. Qadir squeezed her tight until she shoved him away.

"I can't," she told him. "This will never work."

"Why not?"

"I'm a mechanic. I can't go from that to being a princess."

"Why not?"

"You need someone else. Someone more in keeping with your place in society."

"I want you. Only you. I want to make you so happy, you feel pity for all other women."

A great goal. She was so tempted. She loved him. This was her dream come true.

"I'm scared," she admitted.

"Of me?"

"Of how much I love you."

"We can face our fears together, sweet Maggie. I love you."

She went to him then, because she didn't have a choice. He already had possession of her heart. He might as well take the rest of her, too.

"Forever," he promised before he kissed her. "Now will you stay?"

She smiled. "Just try to get rid of me."

* * * * *

Look for the next book in Susan Mallery's exciting
DESERT ROGUES *miniseries,*
THE SHEIK AND THE BOUGHT BRIDE
coming soon to Silhouette Special Edition
and now, turn the page for a sneak peek at
SWEET TALK
the first book in Susan's new family saga
available from HQN Books in July 2008

Claire Keyes jumped to answer the phone when it rang, deciding an angry phone call from her manager was more appealing than sorting the pile of dirty clothes in the middle of her living room.

"Hello?"

"Hi. Um, Claire? It's Jesse."

Not her manager, Claire thought, relieved. "Jesse who?"

"Your sister."

Claire kicked aside a blouse and sank onto the sofa. "Jesse?" she breathed. "It's really you?"

"Uh-huh. Surprise."

Surprise didn't begin to describe it. Claire hadn't seen her baby sister in years. Not since their father's funeral, when Claire had tried to connect with the only family she had left only to be told that she wasn't welcome, would never be welcome and that if she was hit by a bus neither Jesse nor Nicole, Claire's fraternal twin, would bother to call for help.

Claire still remembered being so stunned by the verbal attack that she'd actually stopped breathing. She'd felt as if she'd been beaten up and left on the side of the road. Jesse and Nicole were her *family*. How could they reject her like that?

Not knowing what else to do, she'd left town and never returned. That had been seven years ago.

"So," Jesse said with a cheer that seemed forced. "How are you?"

Claire shook her head, trying to clear it, then glanced at the messy apartment. There were dirty clothes piled thigh-high in her living room, open suitcases by the piano, a stack of mail she couldn't seem to face and a manager ready to skin her alive if that would get her to do what they wanted.

"I'm great," she lied. "And you?"

"Too fabulous for words. But here's the thing. Nicole isn't."

Claire tightened her grip on the phone. "What's wrong with her?"

"Nothing…yet. She's going to have surgery. Her gallbladder. There's something weird about the placement or whatever. Anyway, she can't have that easy kind of surgery with the tiny incisions. The lapi-something."

"Laparoscopic," Claire murmured absently, eyeing the clock. She was due at her lesson in thirty minutes.

"That one. Instead, they're going to be slicing her open like a watermelon, which means a longer recovery time. With the bakery and all, that's a problem. Normally, I'd step in to help, but I can't right now. Things are…complicated. So we were talking and Nicole wondered if you would like to come back home and take care of things. She would really appreciate it."

Home, Claire thought longingly. She could go home. Back

to the house she barely remembered but that had always figured so prominently in her dreams.

"But I thought you and Nicole hated me," she whispered, wanting to hope but almost afraid to.

"We were upset. Before. It was an emotional time. Seriously, we've been talking about getting in touch with you for a while now. Nicole would have, um, called herself, but she's not feeling well and she was afraid you'd say no. She's not in a place to handle that right now."

Claire stood. "I would never say no. Of course I'll come home. I really want to. You're my family. Both of you."

"Great. When can you get here?"

Claire looked around at the disaster that was her life and thought about the angry calls from Lisa, her manager. There was also the master class she was supposed to attend and the few she had to teach at the end of the week.

"Tomorrow," she said firmly. "I can be there tomorrow."

"Just shoot me now," Nicole Keyes said as she wiped down the kitchen counters. "I mean it, Wyatt. You must have a gun. Do it. I'll write a note saying it's not your fault."

"Sorry. No guns at my house."

None in hers, either, she thought glumly, then tossed the dishcloth back into the sink.

"The timing couldn't be worse for my stupid surgery," she muttered. "They're telling me I can't go back to work for six weeks. *Six.* The bakery isn't going to run itself. And don't you dare say anything about me asking Jesse. I mean it, Wyatt."

Her soon-to-be ex-brother-in-law held up both hands. "Not a word from me, I swear."

She believed him. Not because she thought she frightened him, but because she knew he understood that while some of the pain in her gut came from an inflamed gallbladder, most of it was about her sister Jesse's betrayal.

"I hate this. I hate my body turning on me this way. What have I ever done to it?"

Wyatt pushed out a chair at the table. "Sit. Getting upset isn't going to help."

"You don't actually know that."

"I can guess."

She plopped into the chair because it was easier than fighting. Sometimes, like now, she wondered if she had any fight left in her.

"What am I forgetting?" she asked. "I think I've gotten everything done. You remembered that I can't take care of Amy for a while, right?"

Amy was his eight-year-old daughter. Nicole looked after her a few afternoons a week.

Wyatt leaned forward and put his hands on her forearm. "Relax," he told her. "You didn't forget anything. I'll look in on the bakery every couple of days. You've got good people working for you. Everything will be fine. You'll be home in a few days and you can start healing."

She knew he meant from more than just the surgery. There was also the issue of her soon-to-be ex-husband.

Instead of thinking about that bastard Drew, she stared at Wyatt's hand on her arm. He had big hands—scarred and calloused. He was a man who knew how to work for a living. Honest, good-looking, funny.

She raised her gaze to his dark eyes. "Why couldn't I have fallen in love with you?" she asked.

He smiled. "Back at you, kid."

They would have been so perfect together…if only there had been a hint of chemistry.

"We should have tried harder," she muttered. "We should have slept together."

"Just think about it for a minute," he told her. "Tell me if it turns you on."

"I can't." Honestly, thinking about having sex with Wyatt kind of set her teeth on edge, and not in a good way. He was too much like a brother. If only his stepbrother, Drew, had caused the same reaction. Unfortunately, with him, there had been fireworks. The kind that burned.

She pulled back and studied Wyatt. "Enough about me. You should get married again."

He reached for his mug of coffee. "No, thanks."

"Amy needs a mother."

"Not that badly."

"There are great women out there."

"Name one that isn't you."

Nicole thought for a minute, then sighed. "Can I get back to you on that?"

The Keyes' bakery had been in the same location for all of its eighty years of operation. Originally, Claire's great-grandparents had rented only half the storefront. Over time, the business had grown. They'd bought out their neighbor's lease, then had bought the whole place about sixty years ago.

Pastries, cakes and breads filled the lower half of the two display windows. Delicate lettering listing other options covered the top half. A big sign above the door proclaimed, "Keyes Bakery—Home of the world's best chocolate cake."

The multilayer chocolate confection had been praised by royalty and presidents, served by brides and written into several celebrity contracts as a "must have" on location shoots or backstage at concerts. It was about a billion calories of flour, sugar, butter, chocolate and a secret ingredient passed on through the family. Not that Claire knew what it was. But she would. She was confident Nicole would want to tell her immediately.

Taking a deep breath, she walked into the bakery.

It was midafternoon and relatively quiet. Claire offered a smile as she made her way to the long counter. The teenage girl there looked at her.

"Can I help you?"

"Yes. I hope so. I'm Claire. Claire Keyes."

The teenager, a plump brunette with big, brown eyes, sighed. "Okay. What can I get you? The rosemary garlic bread is hot out of the oven."

Claire smiled hopefully. "I'm Claire Keyes," she repeated.

"Heard that the first time."

Claire pointed to the sign on the wall. "Keyes, as in Nicole's sister."

The teenager's eyes got even bigger. "Oh my God. No way. Are you really? The piano player?"

Claire winced. "Technically, I'm a concert pianist." A soloist, but why quibble? "I'm here because of Nicole's surgery. Jesse called and asked me to—"

"Jesse?" The girl's voice came out as a shriek. "She didn't. Are you kidding? Oh my God! I can't believe it." The teenager backed up as she spoke. "Nicole is going to kill her. If she hasn't already. I just…" She held up her hand. "Wait here, okay? I'll be right back."

Before Claire could say anything, the girl took off toward the back.

Claire adjusted her bag on her shoulder and looked at the inventory in the glass case. There were several pies, a couple of cakes, along with loaves of bread. Her stomach growled, reminding her she hadn't eaten all day. She'd been too nervous to have anything on the plane.

Maybe she could get some of that rosemary garlic bread and then stop at a deli for—

"What the hell are you doing here?"

Claire looked at the man walking toward her. He was big and rough-looking, with tanned skin and the kind of body that said he either did physical work for a living or spent too much time at a gym. She did her best not to wrinkle her nose at the sight of his plaid shirt and worn jeans.

"I'm Claire Keyes," she began.

"I know who you are. I asked you why you were here."

"Actually, you asked me why the *hell* I was here. There's a difference."

He narrowed his gaze. "Which is?"

"One question implies a genuine interest in the answer, the other lets me know that somehow I've annoyed you. You don't actually care why I'm here, you just want me to know I'm not welcome. Which is strange, considering you and I have never met."

"I'm friends with Nicole. I don't have to have met you to know all I need about you."

Ouch. Claire didn't understand. If Nicole was still mad at her, why had Jesse called and implied otherwise? "Who *are* you?"

"Wyatt Knight. Nicole is married to my stepbrother."

Nicole got married? When? To whom?

A deep, deep sadness followed the questions. Her own sister hadn't bothered to tell her or invite her to the wedding. How pathetic was that?

Emotions chased across Claire Keyes's face. Wyatt didn't bother to try to read them. Women and what they felt were a mystery best left unsolved by mortal man. Trying to make sense of the female mind would drive a man to drink, then kill himself.

Instead, he studied the tall, slender blonde in front of him, looking for similarities to Nicole and Jesse.

Their eyes, he thought, taking in the big, blue irises. Maybe the shape of the mouth. The hair color…sort of. Nicole's was just blond. Claire's was a dozen different colors and shiny.

But nothing else was the same. Nicole was his friend, someone he'd known for years. A pretty enough woman, but regular-looking. Claire dressed in off-white—from her too-long coat to the sweater and slacks she wore underneath. She looked like an ice princess…an evil one.

"I'd like to see my sister," Claire said firmly. "I know she's just been admitted to the hospital. But I'm not sure which one."

"No way I'm going to tell you. I don't know why you're here, lady, but I can tell you Nicole doesn't want to see you."

"That's not what I heard."

"From who?"

"Jesse. She said Nicole was going to need help after her surgery. She called me yesterday and I flew in this morning." She raised her chin slightly. "I'm not going away, Mr. Knight, and you can't make me. I *will* see my sister. If you choose not to give me the information, I'll simply call every hospital in Seattle until I find her. Nicole is my family."

"Since when?" he muttered, recognizing the stubborn angle of her chin and the determination in her voice. The twins had that much in common.

He swore under his breath. "Where are you staying?"

"At the house. Where else?"

"Fine. Stay there. Nicole will be home in a couple of days. You can take this up with her then."

"I'm not waiting two more days to see her."

Selfish, spoiled, egotistic, narcissistic. Wyatt remembered

Nicole's familiar list of complaints about her sister. Right now every one of them made sense to him.

"Listen," he said. "You can wait at the house or fly back to Paris or wherever it is you live."

"New York," she said quietly. "I live in New York."

"Whatever. My point is you're not going to see Nicole until she's had a couple of days to recover, even if that means I have to stand guard outside her hospital room myself. You got that? She's in enough hurt right now from the surgery without having to deal with a pain in the ass like you."

* * * * *

Enjoy a sneak preview of
MATCHMAKING WITH A MISSION
by B.J. Daniels,
part of the WHITEHORSE, MONTANA *miniseries.*
Available from Harlequin Intrigue
in April 2008.

Nate Dempsey has returned to Whitehorse to uncover the truth about his past...

Nate sensed someone watching the house and looked out in surprise to see a woman astride a paint horse just on the other side of the fence. He quickly stepped back from the filthy second-floor window, although he doubted she could have seen him. Only a little of the June sun pierced the dirty glass to glow on the dust-coated floor at his feet as he waited a few heartbeats before he looked out again.

The place was so isolated he hadn't expected to see another soul. Like the front yard, the dirt road was waist-high with weeds. When he'd broken the lock on the back door, he'd had to kick aside a pile of rotten leaves that had blown in from last fall.

As he sneaked a look, he saw that she was still there, staring at the house in a way that unnerved him. He shielded his eyes from the glare of the sun off the dirty window and studied her, taking in her head of long blond hair that feathered out in the breeze from under her Western straw hat.

She wore a tan canvas jacket, jeans and boots. But it was the way she sat astride the brown-and-white horse that nudged the memory.

He felt a chill as he realized he'd seen her before. In that very spot. She'd been just a kid then. A kid on a pretty paint horse. Not this one—the markings were different. Anyway, it couldn't have been the same horse, considering the last time he had seen her was more than twenty years ago. That horse would be dead by now.

His mind argued it probably wasn't even the same girl. But he knew better. It was the way she sat the horse, so at home in a saddle and secure in her world on the other side of that fence.

To the boy he'd been, she and her horse had represented freedom, a freedom he'd known he would never have—even after he escaped this house.

Nate saw her shift in the saddle, and for a moment he feared she planned to dismount and come toward the house. With Ellis Harper in his grave, there would be little to keep her away.

To his relief, she reined her horse around and rode back the way she'd come.

As he watched her ride away, he thought about the way she'd stared at the house—today and years ago. While the smartest thing she could do was to stay clear of this house, he had a feeling she'd be back.

Finding out her name should prove easy, since he figured she must live close by. As for her interest in Harper House… He would just have to make sure it didn't become a problem.

* * * * *

Be sure to look for
MATCHMAKING WITH A MISSION
and other suspenseful Harlequin Intrigue stories,
available in April
wherever books are sold.

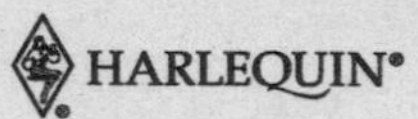

INTRIGUE

WHITEHORSE MONTANA

No matter how much Nate Dempsey's past haunted him, McKenna Bailey couldn't keep him off her mind. He'd returned to town to bury his troubled youth—but she wouldn't stop pursuing him until he was working on the ranch by her side.

Look for

MATCHMAKING WITH A MISSION

BY

B.J. DANIELS

Available in April wherever books are sold.

www.eHarlequin.com

HI69320

Silhouette®

SPECIAL EDITION™

Introducing a brand-new miniseries

Men of Mercy Medical

Gabe Thorne moved to Las Vegas to open a new branch of his booming construction business—and escape from a recent tragedy. But when his teenage sister showed up pregnant on his doorstep, he really had his hands full. Luckily, in turning to Dr. Rebecca Hamilton for the medical care his sister needed, he found a cure for himself....

Starting with

THE MILLIONAIRE AND THE M.D.

by *TERESA SOUTHWICK,*

available in April wherever books are sold.

Visit Silhouette Books at www.eHarlequin.com SSE24894

REQUEST YOUR FREE BOOKS!

2 FREE NOVELS PLUS 2 FREE GIFTS!

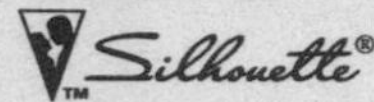

SPECIAL EDITION®

Life, Love and Family!

YES! Please send me 2 FREE Silhouette Speãal Edition® novels and my 2 FREE gifts (gifts are worth about $10). After receiving them, if I don't wish to receive any more books, I can return the shipping statement marked "cancel." If I don't cancel, I will receive 6 brand-new novels every month and be billed just $4.24 per book in the U.S. or $4.99 per book in Canada, plus 25¢ shipping and handling per book and applicable taxes, if any*. That's a savings of at least 15% off the cover price! I understand that accepting the 2 free books and gifts places me under no obligation to buy anything. I can always return a shipment and cancel at any time. Even if I never buy another book from Silhouette, the two free books and gifts are mine to keep forever.

235 SDN EEYU 335 SDN EEY6

Name (PLEASE PRINT)

Address Apt. #

City State/Prov. Zip/Postal Code

Signature (if under 18, a parent or guardian must sign)

Mail to the **Silhouette Reader Service:**

IN U.S.A.: P.O. Box 1867, Buffalo, NY 14240-1867

IN CANADA: P.O. Box 609, Fort Erie, Ontario L2A 5X3

Not valid to current subscribers of Silhouette Speãal Edition books.

Want to try two free books from another line?

Call 1-800-873-8635 or visit www.morefreebooks.com.

* Terms and prices subject to change without notice. N.Y. residents add applicable sales tax. Canadian residents will be charged applicable provinãal taxes and GST. This offer is limited to one order per household. All orders subject to approval. Credit or debit balances in a customer's account(s) may be offset by any other outstanding balance owed by or to the customer. Please allow 4 to 6 weeks for delivery. Offer available while quantities last.

Your Privacy: Silhouette is committed to protecting your privacy. Our Privacy Policy is available online at www.eHarlequin.com or upon request from the Reader Service. From time to time we make our lists of customers available to reputable third parties who may have a product or service of interest to you. If you would prefer we not share your name and address, please check here. ☐

SSE08

Family crises, old flames and returning home... Hannah Matthews and Luke Stevens discover that sometimes the unexpected is just what it takes to start over...and to heal the heart.

SHERRYL WOODS

On sale March 2008!

SAVE $1.00 **on the purchase price of SEAVIEW INN by Sherryl Woods.**

Offer valid from March 1, 2008, to May 31, 2008.
Redeemable at participating retail outlets. Limit one coupon per purchase.

Canadian Retailers: Harlequin Enterprises Limited will pay the face value of this coupon plus 10.25¢ if submitted by customer for this product only. Any other use constitutes fraud. Coupon is nonassignable. Void if taxed, prohibited or restricted by law. Consumer must pay any government taxes. Void if copied. Nielsen Clearing House ("NCH") customers submit coupons and proof of sales to Harlequin Enterprises Limited, P.O. Box 3000, Saint John, N.B. E2L 4L3, Canada. Non-NCH retailer—for reimbursement submit coupons and proof of sales directly to Harlequin Enterprises Limited, Retail Marketing Department, 225 Duncan Mill Rd., Don Mills, Ontario M3B 3K9, Canada.

U.S. Retailers: Harlequin Enterprises Limited will pay the face value of this coupon plus 8¢ if submitted by customer for this product only. Any other use constitutes fraud. Coupon is nonassignable. Void if taxed, prohibited or restricted by law. Consumer must pay any government taxes. Void if copied. For reimbursement submit coupons and proof of sales directly to Harlequin Enterprises Limited, P.O. Box 880478, El Paso, TX 88588-0478, U.S.A. Cash value 1/100 cents.

® and TM are trademarks owned and used by the trademark owner and/or its licensee.
© 2008 Harlequin Enterprises Limited

MSW2529CPN

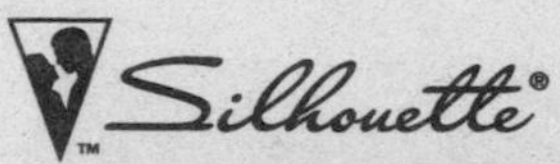

SPECIAL EDITION®

COMING NEXT MONTH

#1891 ONCE UPON A PREGNANCY—Judy Duarte
The Wilder Family
The home pregnancy test results were in—nurse Simone Garner was carrying Mike O'Rourke's baby. More than once, the sexy paramedic had implied that he wanted to start a family and that Simone would make the perfect wife. But would she get cold feet…or was she ready to take baby steps to the altar?

#1892 FINDING FAMILY—Gina Wilkins
All the pieces were falling into place for Dr. Mark Thomas—a coveted partnership in private practice, a new dream house, even a long-lost brother connecting him to the family he thought he'd lost. Then Rachel Madison entered the picture—and soon it became crystal clear that the ravishing interior decorator had designs on him, too!

#1893 BABY, I'M YOURS—Karen Templeton
Guys and Daughters
After a bout with substance abuse, Kevin Vaccaro traveled cross-country to New Mexico to rediscover himself…and discovered he was the daddy of a four-month-old! The baby's aunt and guardian, Julianne McCabe, was wary about having Kevin back in the picture, but couldn't help being attracted to this man on the mend.…

#1894 THE MILLIONAIRE AND THE M.D.—Teresa Southwick
Men of Mercy Medical
Gabe Thorne moved to Las Vegas to open a new branch of his booming construction business—and to escape from recent tragedy. But when his teenage sister showed up pregnant on his doorstep, he really had his hands full. Luckily, in turning to Dr. Rebecca Hamilton for the medical care his sister needed, he found a cure for himself.…

#1895 BACHELOR BOSS—Christie Ridgway
Upon returning to her hometown of San Diego, Lucy Sutton agreed to be family friend Carlo Milano's temporary assistant. Now if only her unrequited crush on the older man would go away so she could get some work done! But was said crush more requited than she thought? And would a three-week job turn into a lifetime…of love?

#1896 BABY ON THE RUN—Kate Little
Baby Daze
To escape her romantically obsessed, criminal-minded boss, widow Carey Mooreland took her six-month-old girl, hit the road… and promptly swerved into a ditch! It was police officer Ben Martin to the rescue, but before he got too close to this beautiful woman, he had to find out if she was an innocent victim or her boss's partner in crime.…

SSECNM0308